sugarsnap

I. S. Belle

KDP ISBN: 979-8-398-99061-4

IngramSpark ISBN: 978-0-473-67669-8

author's note

THE BABYLOVE BOOKS are a companion series to the ZOMBABE trilogy. SUGARSNAP happens in between book #1 and book #2 of ZOMBABE.

content warnings

You know the drill! If any of these content warnings squick you out, you might want to take a pass on this one:

Animal death, gore, murder, homophobia, cannibalism, cops, arson.

"Disco is dead. The light remains.
Come and kiss me in the flames.
My love, let's never stop spinning -"

- a dream forgotten upon waking

chapter
one

THE SUMMER of 2004 was infused with the strange, inexplicable feeling that something terrible was going to happen.

This was partly correct. Something terrible had already happened in Bulldeen, and there was more to come—but not yet. In the cafeteria of Bulldeen High, something else was growing. Something sweet and kind. An Eden in the shape of a plastic table.

Frankie didn't notice Ivy until a small, smooth hand stroked her shoulder.

"Jesus!" Frankie jumped, whirling in time to see Ivy's bemused expression, her red lips creasing into a grin.

Frankie sighed. "Sorry. I didn't hear you come up."

"It's fine." Ivy Wexler sat across from her. They used to sit next to each other, but it had raised too many eyebrows. Her sneaker bumped Frankie's boot under the table. "How was English?"

"Ugh. How was AP?"

"*Ugh*," Ivy said, in a decent impression of Frankie's groan.

Frankie Tanner did her best not to look charmed. She turned her boot against Ivy's sneaker and her clean white socks.

Ivy was in her cheerleader uniform again. Up until last year it was a constant sight. Now she only wore it twice a week when she had after-school practice. She was the lone cheerleader who had broken away from her squad's table to sit with Loser Tanner in their little corner.

The cheerleader table was its usual flurry of white and red skirts. Once upon a time, Frankie's sister, April Tanner, sat with them, making fun of the less popular and stealing people's milk.

"Hey." A crimson nail brushed Frankie's wrist. "You okay?"

"Fine," Frankie said immediately. Like she was going to say anything else in this place. "Heard your squad bitching about getting ash on their shoes from practice. That's bull, right?"

"You've been in the gym! I think it still *smells* like smoke, but everything's intact. *Finally.*"

Frankie hummed in agreement. The gym burned down at the end of their freshman year. Now they were at the start of junior year, and the gym had only just been re-opened after over a year of using the field and canceling gym when it rained. Students complained about a charcoal stench and black streaks on their ankles. Frankie didn't smell anything, and her shoes were always clean after gym. But the room still gave her the creeps.

We know it's a lot to deal with, Principal Skinner had said after he pulled her into his office two weeks ago. *Especially for you, after...what happened. But you can't just not go to class.*

Frankie had seriously considered spitting on him. But she wanted to graduate next year. So she'd gritted her teeth and said, *yes sir.* And she'd walked into the gym and run laps on the floorboards April bled out on.

They still hadn't told her how someone could bleed out during a fire.

7

"Frankie?"

Frankie startled. "What?"

Ivy tugged at her hair. The blonde dye had almost completely grown out, so her hair was light brown except for the ends. "Are you sure you're—?"

A shriek drowned her out. Frankie whirled, heart in her throat.

A cheerleader had her hands over her mouth and was staring teary-eyed down at her footballer boyfriend. In his hands was a sign with the words spelled out in glitter: WILL YOU GO TO HOMECOMING WITH ME?

"Yes," the cheerleader, whose name was Debby, sobbed, as if this was a marriage proposal and not a dance that happened every year. "A thousand times yes!"

She leapt into his arms. Uproarious applause followed from the cheerleaders' table, scattered applause from everywhere else.

The cafeteria soon turned back to its dull chatter. Bulldeen High had been quieter since the gym burned down. It didn't help that the thornfruit fields, Bulldeen's only export and the sole reason the town stayed alive, had died around the same time. People were fleeing in droves as section after section of the thornfruit factory closed down, and businesses went bust. The Homecoming game had been canceled, with too many footballers leaving and no one stepping up to fill their positions.

It wouldn't be long before Bulldeen was a ghost town.

Ivy rolled her eyes at Debby embracing her boyfriend. "She doesn't even *like* him."

"Who would?"

Ivy giggled. "Right? Zit city. Ew." She flipped her hair over her shoulder, and the thought struck Frankie how derisive she would've been about that gesture a year ago. Now all she felt was fondness and longing, both of which she schooled carefully out of her expression as Ivy continued, voice lowering: "Would you do one of those corny proposals, if you could?"

Frankie pressed her lips together to stop her smile from getting out of control. She could feel her black lipstick smudging. She'd have to reapply it before class.

"Why am I proposing?" she whispered. "Where's *my* proposal?"

"Do something to deserve one." Ivy flipped her hair again, taking care to almost hit Frankie in the face, giggling when Frankie scowled. "So? What would you do?"

Their shoes brushed once again under the table. Casual. Almost incidental.

Frankie leaned forward. "I wouldn't do it like that idiot. You don't want something public, in front of everyone."

"I don't?"

"No. You want something private. Secluded. I'd...I don't know, I'd put fairy lights all over your room when you were in the shower and turn all the lights off, and when you came out, I'd be kneeling on the carpet. Or whatever."

Ivy's teasing grin turned soft and knowing. "Would you make me a sign?"

"Yeah, sugarsnap. I'd make you a sign."

They stared at each other under the fluorescent lights. For a moment there were no high schoolers carving circles in tables, no lunch lady calling for more meatloaf, no teachers speaking in hushed tones about another cat found with its throat ripped out. It was just the two of them: Ivy and Frankie, against the world.

Frankie pushed the tip of her boot against Ivy's socks. "Do you wanna—"

"Yes," Ivy said.

As make-out spots went, a high-school toilet stall was not ideal. In their defense, they were 2004-era lesbians in small-town Maine. They couldn't sneak behind the field or find an empty classroom. Any kissing outside of their bedrooms required walls and no windows.

"Just two more years," Ivy said into Frankie's neck. "Then we get the hell out of here. Go to New York."

Frankie nodded. It was hard to think with Ivy's mouth on her neck, Ivy's hands on her waist, Ivy's lavender perfume against her face. She would have agreed to anything. *Flush my head down the toilet? Yes ma'am, whatever you say.*

The door creaked open. Frankie bit down on her lip, silencing her moan.

"—kind of excited to see them die," said Madeline Grisham, who was repeating senior year for the third time. "You know? Like, our parents looove those fields, thornfruit made the town, blah blah. But you can't say there wasn't some satisfaction in watching everything shrivel up and *rot*. Right?"

"Die die die, baby," said Selena Grisham, three years younger than her sister, also in senior year.

The faucets turned on. Water splattered into basins. In their tiny stall, Frankie set her forehead against Ivy's, waiting, Selena's voice on a loop in her head. *Die die die, baby.* It sounded like a song with a name she couldn't remember.

"Kind of disappointing," Madeline continued, the words slurred, as if she was pulling her bottom lip up to check for chin blemishes. "Like, it's just one. But still."

"It's not like rats—can I have that?" Rustling noises of a makeup bag being opened. "Thanks—one might just mean *one*. It's the first that's grown in over a *year*, Mads."

"Yeah, and I was—gimme that, you always use too much— I was *sooo* happy to see it die! Someone should throw a party.

That should be the Homecoming theme: Bulldeen is dying, let's shoot confetti cannons for the funeral."

Ivy's head came up. The fine hair of her brows tickled Frankie's neck as they pulled inwards. Frankie held her breath. The taps stopped. Lips smacked. The sisters had traded lip gloss.

"I hate this goddamn place," said Madeline coldly. "I hope that plant shits itself before the week is up. I hope somebody burns those plants and salts the earth. Free us from this shithole."

Free us, Frankie mouthed against Ivy's cheek. She'd never agreed with Madeline on anything before today.

"Anyway," Madeline sighed. "They found another cat. Throat ripped out. Who do you think—"

"I mean, they're saying it's dogs?"

"It's not *dogs,* ugh. You're such a wasteoid..."

Footsteps. The sisters' chatter died as the bathroom door swung shut.

Frankie let out her breath. Stepped back. "The bell's gonna go. We should—"

Ivy stared at her, face pale.

Frankie's heart thumped. "What?"

Ivy just looked at her.

"It's fine," Frankie said. "It's—it's just one plant. Bulldeen's practically signed its death certificate. This doesn't mean anything. The cats, neither."

Ivy's hand fluttered up to scratch next to her mouth.

"Don't." Frankie caught it. It was Ivy's worry spot, and it had finally started bleeding last year during all the resurrection crap that brought the girls together. It had scabbed for weeks before finally healing over.

Ivy's fingers curled in hers. She squeezed, then went over to the sinks. She wet a paper towel and dabbed Frankie's black lipstick from her face and neck. Frankie busied herself reapplying said lipstick, a thick dark layer to match her hair.

Their eyes met in the mirror.

"It's fine," Frankie said. "We don't even know—it might not have anything to do with all of Bulldeen's...magic shit."

Ivy looked less than convinced. Frankie couldn't blame her. Ivy's granddad's resurrection had been averted right before anything got locked in, but for months after the ritual they had nightmares about the creature. That strange, shapeshifting figure in the corner of the basement, sloughing into the people who had hurt them the most—but never all the way. The face was always too sharp, teeth too long, body too tall.

Then the real resurrection happened. Babe Simmons, a senior, died just before the school year ended. The day of his funeral, he was up and walking around again. The murders started not long after that.

Ivy and Frankie stayed the hell out of it. They stayed away from Babe and his friends, dubbed "The Dead Freaks." They didn't participate in the Zombabe gossip, which only got louder the more bloodshed ramped up. Then everything came to a crescendo: notorious bully Hunter Creel attacked one of the Dead Freaks, set his own friend Moe on fire, burned down the school gym and somehow ended up dying inside it. They heard he attacked the police chief, Kate Higgins. They heard he didn't die of smoke inhalation. That he died of *blood loss*, like April Tanner.

They heard the Dead Freaks, plus Chief Higgins, drove away from the fire like something was after them—or they were after something. They heard the thornfruit fields started dying that same day. They heard Babe Simmons' valedictorian speech was ominous and *weird*, and that he and the Dead Freaks got the hell out of Bulldeen right after.

Frankie and Ivy heard a lot of things. They didn't ask.

Frankie cupped her girlfriend's uncertain face. "Two years," she said. "Then New York."

Ivy nodded, and the trust in her eyes made Frankie's chest throb. The moment was only slightly marred by Frankie's yawn, her jaw cracking.

"Tired baby," Ivy cooed. Frankie swatted at her.

Sincerity crept into Ivy's tone. "Bad dreams?"

Rotting thornfruit fields stretching beyond the horizon. Sharp, familiar cheekbones. Strange songs, the lyrics forgotten upon waking. Guilt rising like smoke, thick enough to choke.

"Nope," Frankie said, popping the P. It was a lie, and they both knew it. But Ivy nodded, the two of them sharing another moment of being *FrankieandIvy* before heading back out into the world—

—and straight into Marvin Martin, mediocre footballer, perpetual polo shirt wearer, and Ivy's ex-boyfriend.

"Jesus," Frankie spat, reeling back. "Watch where you're going, asshole."

Marvin smiled tightly, and Frankie caught up: he'd been *standing* outside the girl's bathroom, not walking by.

Fear and anger rolled through her in equal measure. She prepared an eyeroll and a growl, and failing that, the knife she kept in her back pocket.

"Always found it weird, girls going to the bathroom together," Marvin drawled.

"I always found it weird when boys stand outside girls' bathrooms," Frankie replied flatly. "Scram, Marvin."

Marvin's gelled hair stayed perfectly still as he cocked his head. "You know what? *I* think what's weird is you girls spending *twenty minutes* in there."

Shit. Frankie opened her mouth, but Ivy beat her to it.

"Women's troubles," she said, sweetness ringed with venom. *There* was the cheerleader Frankie used to loathe, repurposed to defend her girlfriend. "You wouldn't understand. I seem to remember you screaming like a little girl that time you found a tampon in my purse. Did I ever tell you about that, Frankie?"

"No, you did not."

"He *shrieked*, Frankie."

"Did he, Ivy?"

Marvin snarled, "I didn't *shriek*. I was just surprised. You shouldn't keep those things lying around where unsuspecting guys can see them."

He stepped in close to Ivy. Frankie's hand locked around the knife in her pocket. If this little shit tried anything...

"Are you high?" He scanned Ivy's face worriedly. "Did she get you high, Ives?"

Frankie laughed. "Oh my god, leave us *alone*."

"Don't call me Ives," Ivy said, and took Frankie's wrist. "Let's go."

Marvin called her name down the hall. Ivy didn't stop until they were around the corner.

"He's so *annoying*," she barked. "I can't believe him. Am I high? I'm at *school*!"

The bell rang. Students streamed around them.

The girls set off for English. Their hands bumped, incidental. Frankie kept her eyes ahead and told herself Marvin was the biggest thing they had to worry about, Marvin and not being able to go to Homecoming together, Marvin and this homework assignment coming up she hadn't started yet.

Marvin was their worst threat, she assured herself, as they slid into their seats on opposite sides of the room. Nothing else.

chapter
two

IVY'S HOUSE was the same as ever: clean, beautiful, and utterly unlived in.

Frankie ran her finger along a windowsill. No dust. Around the corner was the kitchen, where Ivy was arguing yet again why she should be allowed to take dinner to her room. It was a well-worn fight. Frankie didn't know why her parents insisted on having it. Whenever Frankie was wrangled to the dinner table, they spent the whole time watching her like she was going to steal the silver, maybe plunge one of their precious forks into their throats.

"I just think it's rude," came Mrs. Wexler's voice from the kitchen. Frankie could picture her leaning against the countertop with her pristine blouse and honest-to-god pearls. "I make her dinner and she doesn't even want to eat with us. What kind of guest is she?"

"Gee, mom, I don't know. A guest who's suffered through that dinner a dozen times? *She's* fine with coming down—"

"Sure she is."

"—*I* just can't take her pretending to be interested in the round the table talk! *How was your day? Good, and you? Good.*

Oh, that's good. And then we just sit in silence! For minutes on end! Excuse me for not wanting to subject my friend to that!"

"Don't raise your voice," Mr. Wexler said. Crunching sounds. He'd broken into his pre-dinner crackers.

"I didn't."

A put-upon sigh. "Ivy, dear. It's nice of you to spend so much time with her, after...what happened. But don't you think you should be able to leave her alone by now? Don't you miss your old friends?"

Frankie rubbed her forehead against the wall. Her hair rasped, trapped between skin and wood.

"No, mom. I really don't."

The fridge opened. Closed. Wine poured into glasses. Frankie imagined Mr. Wexler dunking his cracker in, which he only did to make his wife's nose turn up.

"Marvin called again," said Mr. Wexler through his sour mouthful. "You're really running out of time to find anyone else to ask you to Homecoming."

Frankie closed her eyes.

Ivy's voice was ice-cold. "I'm not going."

"Ivy—"

Footsteps. Frankie opened her eyes as Ivy appeared around the corner and pushed a plate into her waiting hands. They fell into step beside each other and sped down the hall toward sanctuary.

I like the idea of a silent dinner, Frankie told her once. *Like, if everyone's just enjoying each other's company, being...comfortable.*

Ivy had been quiet for a long time before agreeing. The silence the Wexlers lapsed into after every perfunctory cycle of *how was your day* made her pick at her hands. A finger would curl in, hidden by her fork or spoon, and dig into her hand. Her parents had been pleased when her calluses healed in the past year. Evidently, they hadn't noticed the correlation between Ivy's new smooth hands and her absence from the dinner table.

Frankie sat on the floor against the bed. A wilted salad leaf spilled over the plate, sliding onto the carpet.

"Gross," Ivy said as she joined her on the bed. "No, babe, don't—"

Frankie picked the leaf back up, chewing loudly.

Ivy groaned. "See if I kiss you for the next few hours."

Frankie grinned, bumping her knee into Ivy's as they settled into their dinner routine: sitting with their backs against her bed, plates in their laps.

Ivy sliced her dinner into bits. Another thing Frankie found endearing about her: she cut her meal up before she ate it. Did she make fun of Ivy for it? Of course. But she still thought it was cute.

"Any gossip?" Ivy asked.

"Other than that stupid plant news? New suspect on the cat-killer list."

"Didn't you hear? It's *wild dogs.*"

Frankie snorted. These cat killings weren't wild dogs any more than last year's murders were wild dogs.

"So? Who is it this time?"

Frankie leaned her chin on Ivy's shoulder. "Mr. Clack."

Ivy's hand flew to her mouth, catching the slice of steak she'd coughed out. She thumped her chest. "Mr. *Clack*?"

Frankie nodded, as incredulous as Ivy. Mr. Clack was the kindly teacher who had given her a chance to get out of summer school.

Ivy's thudded her head against her bed. "They're accusing *anyone* now. Remember in grade school when Moe Stafford kicked a trash can and his toe split open? Mr. Clack almost threw up. He's not out there biting out cats' throats."

"Mm," said Frankie. She meant to say more, but her brain was caught on a loop.

Moe Stafford was sixteen. He was a whining, cowardly jerk. And he was dead. He was the boy Hunter Creel had doused with gasoline to start the fire in the gym last year.

Out of everybody in that gym, just one person had run to help. One girl had stripped off her shirt and tried to smother the flames: Frankie's sister, April. A mean cheerleader who tried to carve every bit of kindness out of herself. Why hadn't she just let him burn? She didn't even like Moe. Nobody did. She could be so cruel, so unfeeling. Why couldn't she have let that carry her out the gym doors to safety? Their mom was right: kindness really did kill you.

"Frankie?"

Frankie blinked. Ivy's hand was on her knee. When did that happen?

Ivy's smile was hesitant. She held up a green bean. "They gave us sugar snaps."

"Oh, come on." Frankie's heaviness eased, replaced with a fond annoyance only Ivy could induce.

Ivy smirked knowingly. "What? Just a sugar snap."

"Shut up—"

"No, a lot of people get to our age without knowing what a sugar snap is! There's no shame!"

Frankie stole a piece of steak. Ivy gasped, smacking her with her fork.

The sugar snap revelation had happened eight months ago. They'd been in this exact same position, eating dinner from plates in their laps. Ivy had said something about the sugar snaps being too soggy. And Frankie had replied, *the what?*

Sugar snaps, Ivy had said.

Frankie had given her a blank look.

Sugar snaps, Ivy had repeated, holding up a limp bean.

Frankie had poked it with her knife. *What are you talking about? A sugar snap is a wasp.*

After Ivy had stopped laughing and Frankie stopped trying to smother her with a pillow, the story came out: April had told a young Frankie sugar snaps were a vicious breed of wasp, and it had stuck. *A wasp,* Frankie had recited to a giggling Ivy, *that looks like a moth. You only realize what it is after it's stung you. It even sounds violent: sugar-SNAP!*

Ivy had sighed. *I always thought it was a sweet name. I'd hold my own hand and imagine somebody calling me sugarsnap.*

Frankie had linked their fingers together. *Do you like it better than princess?*

I do.

Frankie leaned their foreheads together. *Then howdy, sugarsnap.*

Tonight, Ivy held out the bean. Frankie sucked it into her mouth, chewing neatly. She leaned once more on Ivy's shoulder, twisting to breathe in her lavender scent.

"I like your perfume."

"Thank you," Ivy said softly. "My girlfriend got it for me."

They ate the rest of dinner in comfortable silence, knees knocking. Frankie stacked their plates neatly beside them.

"I'll go down later," she said. She liked running into Ivy's parents in the kitchen. It meant she got to thank them, and they got to see her doing the dishes. You couldn't hate a teenager who voluntarily washed dishes.

Ivy twisted her skull ring. Once it belonged to Frankie. Now it sat on Ivy's ring finger, a tiny gleaming badge: *this girl is mine.* It made Frankie want to wear something of Ivy's. She could pull off red. Red could be goth.

"I was thinking," Ivy said, toying with the skull's eyeholes. "In New York, we should grow herbs."

"Herbs?"

"We can't have a garden in an apartment. But we can put a planter box on the windowsill. I was thinking—basil? And parsley? Oh, and mint."

Frankie nodded eagerly. Neither of them knew about mint's habit of taking over whatever pot it was planted in. Bulldeen had no gardens. The toxicity in the soil meant nothing grew except for thornfruit, and even that didn't grow anymore.

"Strawberries," Frankie said.

Ivy's eyes widened. "*Yes*. Why didn't I think of that? Strawberries and...something black. To go with our colors. Are blackberries actually black? I've never seen one."

Frankie shrugged. "Nightshade," she suggested. "That sounds black."

Ivy snorted. "Sure, let's put a deadly plant in with the strawberries."

Frankie grinned. She opened her mouth to suggest black rocks, dark crystals, or charcoal nestling in with the dirt.

Something moved behind Ivy's shoulder.

Frankie' stomach lurched.

A figure stood in the corner. Brown hair. Sharp cheekbones —like the monster, yes. But also like a Tanner.

April Tanner raised a hand. Her stomach was a bright red hole, dripping viscera. Her lips curved to form silent words: *you know where to find me.*

"Frankie? What's wrong?"

Frankie jerked. Ivy's hand stopped midway to her face.

Frankie glanced back. No April. No blood on the carpet.

"Nothing." She tried to smile, fighting down the guilt and worry that threatened to choke her. "You're here. I'm good."

Ivy's hand still hovered, unsure. Frankie took it, pressing it into her face, breathing in the floral scent that sent her to sleep two nights a week, the limit she was allowed to stay over. In New York they'd have every night. In New York they'd have a room where they didn't have to inflate an air mattress every night, maintaining the ruse. No rolling out of bed if Ivy's parents knocked. Just a double bed and Ivy's lavender-scented skin against Frankie's face as they fell toward sleep.

chapter
three

"I JUST WANT to start by saying you're a pig."

Chief Kate Higgins stared blearily at Frankie from her front door. It was 8 a.m. on a Saturday. Her T-shirt was riddled in old stains: coffee, whiskey, a dark dry spot that looked like blood. She was wearing boxers. Frankie had never seen a woman in boxers before. She didn't know it was allowed.

"Alright," Kate said dryly.

Frankie tore her gaze away from the boxers. She'd had a whole speech planned. She wasn't going to walk into a cop's house and start talking without giving her a piece of her mind first.

"Cops, I mean." How did the next part go again? "Like, as a system. You guys oppress people for the ruling class."

"Alright," Kate repeated. She scratched the wedge of belly sticking out between her shirt and boxers. Her face hadn't changed from the eternal expression Frankie called: *I'm too tired for this shit.*

Frankie cleared her throat, cheeks reddening under her pale foundation. "You're, um. Taking this better than I expected."

"Would you like me to get burned up about it? Cause I can

pretend." Kate yawned. She didn't even cover her mouth. Gold fillings gleamed near her throat. "Why are you here, Tanner?"

Frankie sucked in a breath. "Everybody says you were involved in the...Babe thing. The Dead Freaks thing."

Kate reached for the doorknob. "You know I don't talk about that."

Frankie's foot shot out, boot catching the door before it could swing closed. "I think you should."

Kate gave her another weary look. "Or what?"

"I just...think you should."

Maybe it was Kate witnessing Babylove's bullet-ridden corpse last year. Maybe it was April's horrible death. Maybe it was how Frankie's voice broke. Whatever it was, Kate stared at her a moment longer, lips a thin white line.

The door creaked open. Kate jerked her head. "Inside."

Frankie followed Kate into the living room, politely not wrinkling her nose at the stale musk: decades of booze and nicotine and sweat layered on top of each other.

Kate vanished into the hallway and came back wearing pants. She hesitated, before pulling over a battered armchair, then motioned for Frankie to sit on an even more battered couch. Frankie got the feeling she didn't get many visitors. No need to worry about seating arrangements.

Kate lit up a cigarette. Took a long, hard pull. "Okay, go."

"What *happened*? Something ripped out her liver. That wasn't Hunter."

Kate's mouth twisted around her mouthful of smoke. "Who the hell told you that?"

"Does it matter?"

Kate stared at her dully.

"A few dickheads said weird shit to me in the halls, Like, weirder than usual. One day I—I shoved some asshole into his locker and asked for the full story. He said she was missing, like, most of her torso. And when I asked the coroner's daughter, she said that too."

"Mm. Shove her into a wall?"

"No, I cornered her in the Shop N' Save."

"Mm." Kate took another suck on her cigarette. Smoke drifted out her nostrils. Frankie scratched her dull nails against her tights, watching the smoke drift up to the yellow ceiling.

"Hunter was very sick."

Frankie scoffed. "Don't bullshit me, *Hunter* wasn't the one biting out people's throats last summer."

"Shit, *Babe* didn't do that to your sister. He's a good kid."

A quiet sting. Frankie looked down. She'd dug a hole in her tights, her blunt black nails scratching a red line into her knee.

She wedged her hands under her skirt. "Say I saw something. Say I talked to...something. Say I know Bulldeen is...bad. Unnatural."

Kate was a woman of few expressions. Even with her mind whirring, Frankie only got the briefest glimpses: a tense jaw. A too-fast blink. Downturned eyes, just for a moment, before they raised once again to meet Frankie head-on.

"Whatever you talked to," Kate said gruffly, "it's dead."

"You're sure?"

"I'm sure."

"You and the Dead Freaks killed it?"

Kate leaned forward, dirty blonde hair falling in front of her eyes. Frankie had never seen it out of its ponytail before. "Your sister tried to help Moe. In the gym."

"I know. That was the only other thing the officer would tell me." Frankie averted her eyes. *It's the kindness that kills you.* A catchphrase their mom passed down to her daughters. It was by no means the last thing April said to her—they had weeks in between that talk and April bleeding out in the gym—but when Frankie pictured the last time she saw her, she thought of April's bitter smile around those familiar words.

Kate took another drag. "I'm sorry this happened," she said slowly, like she was searching for better words and couldn't find any. "But you should let her rest."

Frankie blinked. A mascara-heavy eyelash caught on her cheek. She picked it off. Black smudges on her finger transferred to her knee when she went back to picking through the hole in her tights.

"I'm not—" Frankie's cheeks burned. "I'm not going to... do anything."

Frankie felt the pressure of Kate's gaze and ducked her head. Tried to look deep in thought, which wasn't hard. Tried to look innocent, which wasn't a natural state for her. Frankie had sunk years into looking as if she was moments away from a felony. The knife helped. She thought about getting it out of her skirt pocket. Part of her wanted to see Kate's reaction.

"Does your girl know you're here?"

It caught Frankie off guard. She looked up. "My what?"

"Your other half. Don't think I've seen you two apart once in the last year."

Frankie couldn't tell if she was joking. All of Kate's jokes—and they were few and in between—were said in that same dry tone.

"We're best friends."

Kate's mouth twisted around her cigarette. Almost a smile. She hesitated. Tapped ash into the carpet. "I had a friend like that once."

Frankie's heart pounded. That couldn't mean what she thought it meant. But—the *hesitation*. The careful casualness. The fact that Kate Higgins had never had a boyfriend in her life. Holy shit, was their police chief a lesbian?

Frankie made sure her voice was the same careful brand of casual. "What happened?"

"She got out of here. Like anyone with a brain." Kate tapped her cigarette on the couch. More ash on the carpet. She owned an ashtray. Frankie could see it over on the coffee table. It was piled high with gray.

Kate flexed her shoulders. Even reeling with the morning's revelations, Frankie tracked the movement: there was always something strange and scary and satisfying about watching Chief Higgins move. As a child Frankie would watch her crossing the street, waiting in line at the bakery, rooting around the frozen food section: solid shoulders, soft pouchy stomach, her clothes forever plain and unassuming. She never smiled unless she meant it, and she rarely meant it.

Kate gave another flex. Frankie watched the line of her shoulders. It wasn't attraction, not quite—it was recognition. Possibility. *Women can exist like that?* Watching Kate gave Frankie the same feeling as smoothing on black lipstick in the mirror, pulling on her leather jacket and thick boots, slathering her hair in dark dye, slipping a knife into her skirt pocket.

"Anything else?" Kate said. "Or can I get back to my busy morning of recovering from this hangover?"

If Frankie was older, she would have pried. At 25, even at 18, she would have found a way to probe further. But she was 16. It was 2004. She'd never met another confirmed lesbian before, except for Ivy.

"Frankie."

Frankie startled. "No. That's...that's it."

"Okay." Kate nodded at the door.

Frankie got up. Near the door, she stopped. Turned around. Thought once more about asking. Then she left.

Your girl. Your girl. Your girl. It beat a pulse behind Frankie's ribcage. It was so loud she didn't notice the footsteps until they were almost on top of her.

"Loser Tanner!"

Frankie's hand shot into her pocket, fingers wrapping around her knife.

Marvin jogged up. His lip was curled. He found her off-putting and pathetic when she was an ugly smear on his high school landscape. Now she'd turned his ex-girlfriend against him, she was a threat.

Frankie bared her teeth. "*What*, Marvin?"

Marvin frowned at her. A stupid, put-on frown like she didn't know exactly what he was thinking.

"A guy can't come up and say hi?"

"No, he can't. What do you want?"

Marvin frowned at her some more. Frankie imagined lighting his gelled hair on fire, those frosted tips going up in smoke. Couldn't fake an expression with your head on fire.

Marvin sniffed. Spat on the concrete. He didn't use enough force, so some of it dripped down his chin. He wiped at it fast. Marvin was not a spitting man.

"Found a date to the Homecoming dance yet?"

Frankie laughed. She couldn't help it. "Aw, you wanna ask me, Marv?"

"You wish. I just heard Ivy won't go unless you go. Which means you're still tragically un-asked."

"What? Who's saying that?"

"Doesn't matter. So it's true? You and Ivy—"

"None of your business."

He glared at her. "You know they're going to kick her off the cheerleading squad because of you, right?"

"We don't even have football games to cheer for anymore,"

Frankie said, once her brain had caught up. "Cheer squad's gonna end whether she's in it or not."

She noticed the pointed looks the cheer squad gave her and Ivy's little table. How could she not? The worry had been there in the back of her head, even when Ivy laughed it off. *They won't kick me out, Frankie, God. I can hang out with other people. It's not a cult.*

Marvin stepped close. "I don't know what you did to make her think you're worth any of this. But I'm going to save her."

"Good luck." Frankie's neck itched. She looked over Marvin's shoulder, then her own. Nothing but empty houses in a rotting suburb.

"Excuse you?" Marvin snapped his fingers in front of her face. "Do you have something better to do?"

Anger ripped through Frankie like wildfire. "Better than talking to you? Eating *roadkill* is better than talking to you, Marvin. Get out of my way."

She shoved past him. There were still moments where he backed down, intimidated, and she treasured them like little jewels. Then, sometimes—

Marvin grabbed her elbow.

"What the hell?" Frankie yanked. His grip stayed fast. Frankie's arm went white with pressure marks.

Frankie pulled again. "Ow! Let GO!"

Marvin swallowed. "I know it's you killing all those cats." Marvin's face was white, almost horrified—no, disgusted. He really believed it.

"They have their throats ripped out." Frankie flashed her teeth. "Think I have the fangs for it?"

"I heard what happened to Babylove," Marvin blurted. "I know what you are."

It should've made Frankie laugh. But all she could think of was Babylove's brain sprawled red over the grass. The

28

screaming kid. Rituals, fake failsafes, wind whipping through the basement and trying to wrench Ivy away from her. *I know what you are*, like a curse. Kate's voice, rough from decades of smoke and booze: *I had a friend like that once.*

"Then you should know I didn't kill him," Frankie croaked. "That was Mrs Gracegood."

Frankie shuddered, unable to stop herself from picturing the horrified face of the woman who'd shot the resurrected cat to protect her toddler.

Marvin frowned. "What? That's—no. Everyone says—"

The surprise loosened his grip. Frankie heaved away from him. He didn't try to grab her again. Just stood there, fingers opening and closing, like he'd fumbled a catch.

Frankie stumbled away, unsheathing her knife. "Remember when I punched you in the face and you cried like a little bitch? You'll cry a *lot* harder if I do anything with this."

The knife glinted in the morning sun, catching Marvin in the eyes. He raised a hand against it.

"You wouldn't," he said uncertainly. "We'd destroy you."

"We?"

"The town," he said, like it was obvious. "Someone like you comes after someone like me? Come on, Tanner."

Frankie stared at him. For a moment she was incredulous: how did he not see there was a whole world out there, a world infinitely bigger than this sinkhole of a town?

Frankie straightened. "If you come after me, I know a girl who'd be *very* upset."

"You're no good for her," Marvin said softly, eyes glittering.

Frankie shrugged. Sweat dripped down her neck. "But who's going to see her today, Marv?"

She walked until the end of the road. Then she ran. That feeling, the itch of being watched, stayed until she closed Ivy's bedroom door behind her.

chapter
four

"REMEMBER WHEN WE WERE KIDS, *and everybody dared each other to go into the fields?"*

Frankie kept walking. The voice followed. Footsteps squelched on rotting thornfruit. The fields went on forever.

"You went in," the voice continued behind her, "and you didn't come out. Not for hours. I found you just before nightfall, covered in dirt and crying. Do you remember?"

"Shut up," Frankie told it.

A low laugh. "Well, I remember. I had to carry you out. Wash the dirt off. Put bandages on all the thorn marks. Do you remember what you kept saying?"

Frankie swallowed.

"Sis? Do you remember—"

"Thank you for finding me," Frankie said, and turned.

April Tanner waved. Flared jeans and a halterneck. The clothes she'd died in.

Frankie averted her eyes. "I...like your outfit."

April did a supermodel pose. "Thanks, sis."

"Cut it out."

"Cut what out?" April dropped the pose. Her hands rested on her hips, one foot coming to rest awkwardly on top of the

other like it did when she was a kid. It was so familiar Frankie ached.

"Look," she said. "I want to believe it's you. I'm just...skeptical."

April snorted. "Shocker."

"Hey, this deserves a little skepticism!" Frankie waved around at the endless rotting fields. "Anyway, I'm—it's good to see you. But you know I'm not...you know."

April balanced on one foot, waiting.

"You know," Frankie repeated.

April's plucked brows raised expectantly. "Do I know?"

The words stuck in Frankie's throat like fish bones, sharp and dangerous. "Bringing you back."

April's lips pursed. "Really? So you're just gonna leave me here in this freaky field? It's so boring!"

"I'm sorry."

"Come oooon. You already—"

Frankie cut her off. "The cost is too high. People would die, *April."*

"Frankie," April whined. Then, all at once: her body went lax. Her expression fell slack, foot falling back into place on the ground.

"April?"

April's lip curled. For a second Frankie thought of Marvin, but then April's mouth formed a word, slow and sluggish.

"D...don't."

A shudder ran up Frankie's back. "Don't what?"

April blinked hard, gaze snapping back to Frankie. Her shoulders came back, smile rushing into place.

"Don't wait," she said. "It's really *boring here."*

"April," Frankie whispered. "Was that you? Are you—"

FRANKIE

Frankie jumped. "What was that?"

"Ignore that," April said, striding closer. "Don't you want to hang out some more? I miss hanging out."

Frankie backed up nervously. "You didn't do it when you were alive."

FRANKIE WAKE UP

"I'm sorry about that," April said. "Hey, want to know why I avoided you at school? I know you always wondered."

Frankie kept backing up. Rotting stalks squished and cracked under her feet. Who was that voice? She should remember. Why couldn't she remember?

FRANKIE I'M HERE YOU'RE ALRIGHT

April was too fast. Her hands closed softly around Frankie's face. "Don't listen to that. Stay here."

Frankie twisted away. That voice, she needed to get to that voice, and everything would be okay.

"Frankie."

FRANKIE

"Ask your girlfriend what her first plan was."

FOLLOW ME BACK OKAY YOU'RE HAVING A—

"—nightmare."

Frankie shot up in bed. Wet sheets locked her in place. She shoved at them.

"It's okay." Ivy's hands were cool and methodical, pulling the eyeliner-smudged sheets away, tucking Frankie's hair behind her ears. "You're okay, baby."

Frankie pushed herself up the bed.

"Everything's fine," Ivy added as Frankie shuffled to the edge of the bed. "Totally fine, my parents didn't even hear you, it was a whimpering nightmare, not a screaming one."

Frankie giggled wetly, dropping her forehead onto her knees. "Yay, whimpering."

"Yay," Ivy echoed. She sat cautiously in place, worrying at her hands.

Frankie reached out and stilled those blunt red nails. "Stop. We're six whole months without a new one."

"Right." Ivy moved her free hand toward her face, where the healed scab next to her mouth left no scar. Frankie caught that one, too.

Ivy paused, looking down at their joined hands. "I didn't even notice."

"Yeah, that's what you have me for."

"And this." Ivy twisted the skull ring. "I don't know why I always go for my skin first."

Frankie entwined their fingers, black on red. Her slick palm slid against Ivy's dry one. She withdrew long enough to wipe against the already ruined sheets, then returned to the handhold.

"I'll change your bed before I go."

Ivy shook her head, shuffling around to lie facing Frankie, both of them out of the wet spot. "I'll do that later. I'm just glad you got some sleep."

Frankie twisted to check the clock. She'd slept for three hours straight. Solid effort. She lay back against the pillow Ivy had arranged under their heads. *Ask Ivy what her first plan was.* What the hell did that mean?

Frankie pulled up a smile. She wasn't going to let her nightmares hook into her. "Get up to anything fun?"

Ivy rolled her eyes. "Homework. And Marvin called, *again*. My parents keep giving me the phone instead of hanging up like I'm *clearly* mouthing."

"Nothing hotter than a guy who won't take no for an answer," Frankie deadpanned, trying to calm her racing heart. *You know they're going to kick her off the cheerleading squad because of you, right?*

Ivy moved closer. Their foreheads pressed together, Frankie's dark fringe against Ivy's bare forehead. Frankie closed her eyes and imagined Ivy in her arms under a disco ball, their dresses collecting light and throwing it all around the gym. Impossible. And yet—and *yet*. They couldn't have all of it, but maybe they could have pieces. A glance. Hands brushing. Maybe a twirl, a full twirl, a fun two-seconds dance between friends. Nothing to see here, officer.

Frankie kept her eyes closed. "Maybe you should call him back."

Movement against her forehead. Ivy was checking her expression. "Why would I ever do that?"

Frankie shrugged. "He's nice to you. And when he gets mean, you can handle him. You use him to get into the dance, then you ditch him and hang with me."

The sheets shifted. Frankie cracked an eye open to find Ivy staring down at her like she was trying to puzzle her out. Frankie had caught a few of those looks from Ivy in the first few weeks of them hanging out, but they were always fleeting, embarrassed, ending as soon as Frankie noticed them.

This Ivy—*her* Ivy—didn't look away. She kept staring until Frankie tugged at the still-blonde ends of her hair, twisting the faint curls. Ivy had stopped using her hair straightener once the roots started to grow out.

"What, are you worried? I'll be there. I'll protect you."

"And when he comes after you?"

"Then you'll protect me." Frankie grinned. It was only a little forced. Dead-April twitching in her dream; Marvin's hand squeezing her arm—it all fell into the background when she imagined Ivy's head on her shoulder, swaying to some dumb song under that gleaming disco ball.

Ivy considered. "Who would you go with?"

"I don't know." Frankie snuggled into Ivy's side. "Some guy I can threaten."

Ivy smoothed an arm down her shoulder. "So anyone, then."

"Maybe hit up the chess club," Frankie said, and put on a deep, gruff voice. "*Which one of you punks wants to take me to the dance?*"

Ivy laughed, loose and gasping and real. Frankie would do all sorts of stupid and dangerous and terrible things for that laugh.

Ivy's laugh was still in her ears when she arrived home, whistling. It was past midday, which meant both her parents were either a) drinking at separate bars or b) drinking at friends' houses. Weekends usually meant the second option (especially since the whole Dead Daughter thing) but either way, it meant Frankie could whistle as loudly as she wanted as she strode down the driveway.

Something small and white sat on the porch. No—it *lay* on the porch.

The whistle died. Gravel stopped crunching under Frankie's boots as she came to a halt.

The white thing was fluffy and rigid. Something dark dripped down the porch steps.

Frankie's chest tightened. She took another step. Then another. Everything in her yelled for her to stop, to turn around and start running. But she had to know.

She reached the bottom stair. From here the collar was visible a silver bell nestled under the unmoving jaw. Under the bell was a red gape. The cat's throat had been ripped out. Blood dripped over the stairs, pooling in a sticky mess in front of Frankie's boot.

35

The puddle was still warm. Frankie watched it creep forward, a numb haze building through her body, climbing her throat.

Blood folded around the tip of Frankie's boot.

Frankie felt her mouth open. A scream filled the air. It took her a moment to recognize it as hers.

chapter
five

FRANKIE AND IVY buried the cat in silence. They picked a spot in the back of the yard, and as Frankie smoothed dirt over the grave she couldn't help thinking of symmetry: this yard a mirror image of Ivy's, both hiding murdered cats near the back fence.

"For a second I thought it was Babylove," Frankie admitted, as they wiped congealing blood off the porch. They'd used up two full rolls of paper towels.

"Me too," Ivy said quietly, dropping another rust-colored wad of paper into a bucket. The next towel came away more pink than red. The one after that with splinters and not much else. The porch was almost dry. They were reaching the limits of what they could do.

Frankie pulled Ivy up to check their work. A dark stain bruised the faded wood.

Frankie sighed. "Well, they wouldn't be able to sell this shithole anyway. Who'd buy in Bulldeen?"

"Are your parents finally having the moving talk?"

The moving talk was on the back of everyone's minds since the thornfruit fields started to fail. Every time another section of the warehouse closed, a fresh batch of people fled. Bulldeen without thornfruit was a death sentence, and the axe was dropping.

Frankie groaned, stretching her arms behind her until her muscles cracked. "Nope."

"Not even a, *after you graduate, we're thinking—*'"

"Nope." Frankie cracked her neck, tossing Ivy a grin when she winced. She scraped her boot against the stain. It came away clean. She scraped again, once, twice. On the third scrape she said, "I think they're planning separate moves."

"Oh. That's—"

"A relief. Except what the hell does that mean for me?" She met Ivy's eyes, the silent question echoing between them: *what does that mean for us?* They were counting on their families staying the next two years, enough time for them to graduate. But what would happen if their families decided to take off before then? Long-distance whispers over landlines for a year, maybe longer, before fleeing to New York?

Ivy leaned closer to Frankie. "Maybe they won't have to move. That one stalk is still going strong." She smiled weakly.

Frankie didn't smile back, lost in worry, dread creeping up her spine. There had to be a reason that stalk had sprouted after a year of dead soil and rot. What if...

Frankie squeezed her eyes shut so hard mascara left butter-flies on her cheeks. She reached up, but Ivy was faster, smoothing them away with her small, soft fingers. She wiped them on the lacy neckline of Frankie's black shirt.

"Thanks," Frankie said dryly.

"Just making it darker." Ivy tinkled her newly clean fingers. She bent her index finger inwards, pressing into the meat of her thumb. "Who do you think is doing this?"

The stain loomed in front of them, trailing down the steps. They'd just wiped it up, but suddenly it looked...old. Like it had been there before them. Like all their scrubbing was just to reveal it.

"Frankie?"

Franke shuddered. "Huh?"

"I asked who you think is doing this." Ivy pressed harder into her thumb, rubbing absently as she stared down.

"I don't know," Frankie said. "Marvin's the first guy who would put a dead cat on my doorstep."

The pressure mark faded from Ivy's thumb as Frankie pulled it free.

"Thanks. Sorry." Ivy tried another smile. This one was flashier, the smile she put on at the top of the cheer pyramid. "Still want me to go to the dance with him?"

Frankie rolled her tongue in her mouth, considering. "I mean, he wouldn't have killed the cat *himself*. He would've just...moved it here. After finding it?"

"Great. *Way* better."

"Means he's a wuss," Frankie said. "Means we can handle him."

Ivy looked unimpressed. Frankie checked no one was peeking over their fences, then used their joined hands to tug her close.

"What? You don't wanna go to the dance, sugarsnap?" She spun Ivy around until the unamused expression gave way to a giggle. Her hair fell around her, dark with light ends, wavy in a way it wasn't allowed to be for years. She spun and spun, dancing circles over the blood stain, which looked even older than before. Old and deep. Like Ivy could plummet straight down and never hit the bottom.

"*Frankie.*"

Frankie looked up. Ivy had stopped spinning. When did that happen?

I. S. Belle

Ivy's blue eyes were trained on hers, concerned. She opened her mouth.

"I'm getting us some water," Frankie said, and fled.

She stood in front of the kitchen sink for as long as she dared. Gripping the edges, she stared into the drain. There was a scary story about a drain, she could almost remember it. Something about whispers. Something about blood. Was that Bulldeen gossip, or something else? Frankie couldn't keep track of all the horrifying Bulldeen gossip she'd been told over the years, and she didn't want to start.

She was finally reaching for the glassware cupboard when voices drifted in from the porch. One was Ivy. The other was low, rough, and familiar.

Frankie rushed outside.

Ivy looked up, sentence cut short, looking almost...guilty? "Frankie! Hi! Chief Higgins got a call about a scream, I was just telling her we didn't hear anything."

Kate Higgins tilted her hat. She wore it sometimes in colder weather. It looked stupid. Kate was not a hat person.

Frankie swallowed. "Who calls the cops over a scream in Bulldeen?"

"It's been known to happen," Kate said.

Frankie scooched into place next to Ivy, thinking of security blankets, worry beads, those dogs they put in cheetah enclosures to keep them calm. "Like she said, we didn't hear anything. Sorry to waste your time."

"Not a waste." Kate still didn't look away from Ivy, who was busy examining her shoes. What the hell had Frankie walked in on? Did Kate know anything about the Babylove crap that went down last year? Did she think Ivy was protecting Frankie, newfound cat-killer? Did she think *Ivy* was

40

killing them? Did Kate know if their throats were really being taken out with teeth or a knife? It sounded like information the chief of police would have.

Before Frankie's armpits could get properly damp, Kate spun on her heel and started down the porch steps.

Frankie let out the quietest sigh of relief, which became the quietest groan when Kate stopped halfway down the driveway.

"You girls going to Homecoming?"

Frankie glanced at Ivy, who looked equally lost.

"Uh," Frankie said. "No one's asked us."

"Leaving it pretty late." Kate checked her watch, as if it had a calendar installed. "The dance is next week."

Ivy said, "We're thinking about Marvin."

Frankie elbowed her. Ivy shook her head: *what?*

Kate turned. Chief Higgins did not do incredulous, but this came pretty close. "Your ex who's obsessed with getting you away from the satanist?"

Frankie groaned. "People need to stop saying that! Satanists have a whole different aesthetic. *God.*"

Kate's thumb smoothed absently over her belt. *Like a trucker,* Frankie's mom said of her once, and Frankie had nodded, trying not to look enthralled at the idea of women wearing belts. It was one of the first accessories she added to her wardrobe when she started venturing into goth territory.

"How about KJ?" said Kate.

"KJ...Duong?" Frankie said unhelpfully. There was no other KJ in Bulldeen. Still, it seemed an odd option—KJ was older, and Frankie couldn't remember the last time they talked. It took her a second to remember if he was even still in school.

Kate nodded. "He wouldn't try anything."

Frankie scrutinized her, but Kate was unreadable as ever. Why did she even care if they were going to the dance? Was she

41

living vicariously through them, giving young dykes the chance she never got?

Something flickered over Kate's shoulder. Frankie's gaze strayed—

Behind Kate, a ghostly figure waved. Frankie bit her cheek to hold in a gasp. Distantly, she was aware of Ivy beside her, telling Kate they'd ask him.

Kate nodded, short and sharp. Conversation over. She started to turn back—then stopped. She'd noticed Frankie's face, even paler than usual. Frankie was sure whatever her expression was doing was weird and awful.

"Anything else you girls wanna say before I head off?"

The ghostly April Tanner cocked a brow. Her stomach was scooped out again, blood drenching her denim jeans.

She didn't say anything, but her raised brow communicated perfectly. *Yeah sis, anything else?*

A light press on Frankie's back. Ivy touching her spine. Frankie could feel her worried gaze, a comforting weight pressing through Kate's probing stare, April's ghoulish grin.

Frankie forced her black lips into a smile. "Nope."

chapter
six

KJ DUONG WAS A SENIOR. He never ate the cafeteria meatloaf. He didn't join in when the popular crowd heckled some poor kid, but neither did he interfere. His parents moved from Vietnam when he was still in the womb. He always looked like he had somewhere better to be, and in the past year he'd started wearing the same gray hoodie every day and smoking in the school parking lot.

This was Frankie's total knowledge of the guy. She had no idea why Kate considered him a good option—not to mention she didn't really trust Kate; a lesbian cop was still a cop—but they were running out of time. The dance was next week.

KJ drew up his shoulders as Frankie approached at lunch. This was sensible. Frankie didn't stride up to people unless it was to growl at them. Frankie slowed down, tried to look friendly, but that just made it look like she was stalking up to him with a menacing, if awkward, smile.

KJ turned to leave, flicking his cigarette down and crushing it with his shoe.

"Wait," Frankie blurted. "I'm not here to...do whatever it is you're afraid of."

KJ paused. He looked at her with the barest hint of nerves, but no fear. She could work with that.

Frankie took a loose cigarette out of her pocket.

He stared at it. "Is it a normal one?"

It took Frankie a second. "Yeah, duh. Can't you tell the difference between this and a joint?"

"I don't do any of that. And I heard you...partake." He took the cigarette between two thin fingers. "Thanks."

Frankie held up a lighter. He leaned into it cautiously, eyeing her like one might eye a feral cat across the street: wary, but not in any immediate danger.

"Since when do you smoke?"

KJ shrugged. He had a very good shrug, smooth and languid, expressing the full depth of his indifference. "Picked it up last year. De-stressing."

"Got a lot to de-stress about?"

KJ smirked. "Doesn't everybody in this town?"

He took a drag. She took a drag. He tapped ash onto the concrete. She tapped ash onto the concrete. He looked around for an exit strategy.

Frankie sucked in a breath. "Do you want to go to Homecoming with me?"

The look he gave her would have been insulting if she actually gave a shit about him. Absolute, total bafflement. It was the most expressive she'd ever seen him.

"It's not a trick," she added as his eyes narrowed. "I don't do that."

It took a long time for him to speak. "Sorry, you're...fine? But I don't like you like that."

She rolled her eyes. "No shit. I don't like you like that either, dude. Higgins told me to ask you."

"Anna? I thought she left town with the rest of the Dead Freaks."

44

"No, *Chief* Higgins."

He stared at her. "*Why?*"

"I don't know, she said you wouldn't, like. Attack me."

"Why would I *attack* you?"

"I don't know, she said you were a safe option!" Frankie flicked her hair out of the way of her cigarette, which had come dangerously close to lighting her fringe on fire. "Look, I can't go if I don't have a date. So."

She shrugged. She wasn't as good at it as KJ. Her shrugs always betrayed how deeply she cared. It was infuriating.

KJ's cigarette burned down in his hand, forgotten. He rolled his shoulders, pulling at the hoodie fabric. It was an old hoodie, worn and frayed. He used to dress better, Frankie was sure—she'd envied his effortless cool in the hallways. Now it was the same gray hoodie and jeans. He'd gotten paler, which was a feat. Now that she thought of it, she hadn't seen him at his usual table with his bland mix of friends—not the popular crowd, but not losers, either. Childhood friends. Habitual friends. Stuck together out of small-town circumstance, not out of want.

"The only time I ever even talked to Chief Higgins..." KJ's gaze ticked up toward her. There, finally, she saw it: fear. Not of *her*, of her knife and her sharp mouth and her strangeness—but fear of *something*. Frankie didn't know what.

He looked away fast, the fear shunted under the usual air of disinterest, and for the first time in her life, Frankie wanted to know more about KJ Duong.

"Wouldn't think it's your scene," he said slowly. "You wanna spike the punch bowl? Wanna *Carrie* some cheerleader when she gets Homecoming queen?"

Frankie sucked her cigarette down to the filter. Dropped it. Crushed it under her boot.

"Ivy wants to go," she said.

"Oh." He opened his mouth again, hovering on the edge of speech before clicking it shut.

Frankie waited. "Is that a yes?"

"What? Yeah. Yes, I'll...I'll take you." KJ put his cigarette to his mouth, blinking twice when he saw how much had burned away. He sucked hard. "Who's she going with?"

"We're working on it," Frankie said, and before she could think better of it, she clapped him hard on the back. "See you Saturday at seven, loverboy."

The slap coincided with another deep inhale. Frankie walked away leaving him choking on smoke, and just as she strode out of earshot, she heard it: a surprised, hacking laugh.

Frankie walked through the halls so fast and so boldly the crowds parted. For a second she could convince herself she was huge and terrifying, not a freaky sophomore with a dead sister and a town full of people who found her off-putting at best and an object of disgust at worst.

They can overlap, she told herself, as she turned the corner to find Marvin penning Ivy in against a locker.

Frankie stormed forward, hand flying into her jeans pocket. She'd almost freed her knife when Ivy met her eyes over Marvin's shoulder.

The smallest headshake. Frankie stumbled to a stop. Classes were changing over, people streaming around her, chatting too loudly for her to hear the low conversation happening between her girlfriend and her girlfriend's shithead ex who wanted Frankie to die in a fire.

At least Ivy didn't look threatened. Just uncomfortable. Marvin was leaning on the locker, arm up near her head, not noticing or caring how tightly Ivy held her backpack in front of her body. Her stiff smile. Her fake laugh, which Frankie only heard around Ivy's parents or her cheer squad, the few of them who still deigned to talk to Ivy outside of practice.

Marvin grinned down at her, because he was an idiot who still couldn't tell the difference between genuine happiness and performance. He ducked in like he was going to kiss her—Frankie got her knife back out—but Ivy twisted in time for the kiss to hit her cheek.

Frankie's boot jittered against the linoleum. Finally, *finally*, Marvin pushed off the locker and disappeared down the hall.

Frankie ran over. Ivy met her in the middle.

"Are you—"

Ivy cut her off. "He'll go with me if I have dinner with his parents next month."

That sounded too easy. "*Just* next month?"

"No, but I'm not going to go more than once." Ivy's smile was thin and fleeting and still more solid than anything she'd shown Marvin. "He'll be lucky if I show up to that one."

"Why bother?"

"Maybe we'll string him along to prom next year. What about KJ?"

"He's down."

"Good. We're set." Ivy took Frankie's hand and twisted it to examine her wristwatch. Her thumb stroked a distracted semicircle down the knob of Frankie's wrist. Frankie looked around to check if anyone was watching, but there were only a few people hurrying past toward their next class.

"Ivy?"

Ivy shook her wavy hair out. It had healed a lot since she'd stopped straightening it every day, but it still frizzed, no matter what she did. It looked cute, despite what her parents—or Marvin—said.

Ivy rubbed her fingers through it so it frizzed up more. "Want to go somewhere?"

The boldness in her voice obviously meant somewhere that wasn't chemistry class.

"Pretty early in the year to ditch," said Frankie. "My grades are actually okay now, thanks to you. Like, Principal Skinner called me an okay student. I don't know..."

"Aw," Ivy said. "Big bad goth afraid of ditching *one* class?"

"I'm not afraid, I just..." She trailed off. Ivy's hand was so warm in hers. They'd done it—they were going to Homecoming. Why not ditch? Sure, that feeling of dread was still there, as it had been last summer, resurfacing after a year of dormancy. *Something terrible is going to happen.* Last summer, it had: Babe Simmons rose from the dead. Frankie believed they'd dodged a bullet, not going through with Ivy's ritual to resurrect her granddad. Then people disappeared, or turned up chewed to bits, and Hunter Creel got wilder than usual and the school got set on fire, and Frankie kept searching the crowd for April until the fire was out, and one of the officers was approaching her with a grave expression.

It had nothing to do with us, Ivy whispered to her that night after she'd cried so hard she couldn't speak. *Whatever happened, it had nothing to do with us.*

Back then it was a comfort. There was no comfort now.

Pressure on her hand. Frankie blinked. Ivy was still in front of her, smile yet to fade.

"We need dresses," she reminded Frankie. "We're running out of time."

We're running out of time.

"Yes," Frankie said, smiling even as her stomach sank. "Right."

chapter
seven

THANKS to the owner of the driving school allowing Frankie
to trade shifts at the admin desk for driving lessons, Frankie
could drive. She just didn't have a license yet.

"This is fun," Frankie croaked, hands shaking around the
steering wheel of Ivy's dad's car. "Right? This is fun. Open
road. Ditching school. I'm having so much fun."

Ivy giggled. She had the window down, cupping air as it
streamed past. "Aren't you supposed to be a rebel?"

"A rebel who likes keeping her insides on the inside. If we
crash at this speed—"

"Then don't hit anything."

They passed a sign: WELCOME TO LITTLE HOLLOW.
Frankie slowed down to match the town's speed limit. Little
Hollow was two towns over from Bulldeen. They'd never make
it back before lunch ended, or even the class after that. This
was a half-day ditch. Frankie hadn't pulled one of those since
last year, when her grades were still circling the drain. Having a
girlfriend to kiss in the bathrooms did wonders for her
attendance.

Ivy walked her fingers on the car door. "KJ owns a tux,
right?"

Frankie shrugged, eyes on the road.

"And he just...agreed."

"He was weirded out. But yeah, he started talking about Kate and then he went yeah, alright."

Ivy hummed. Frankie spared a glance over at her pursed lips, red and beautiful.

"Why the hell is Kate helping us?" said Ivy.

A trickle of sweat trickled down Frankie's back. The stressed itching had stopped once they slowed down, but there was still the sweat from being on that open road. She rubbed against the car seat, smearing sweat into her shirt. *Bet the dress shops will appreciate that.* They'd already checked Ms. Petty's dress shop back in Bulldeen, cleaned out by all the other girls who got in weeks ago. Little Hollow was the nearest town with a mall.

"I think she's like us," Frankie admitted.

"Like what?"

Frankie didn't bother answering, too busy squinting at the names of the shops.

Ivy pointed. "That one. Oh!" She gripped the grab handle above her head as Frankie careened into the parking lot, cutting off two drivers.

"I'm doing my BEST," Frankie yelled at the honking cars. She pulled shakily into a parking spot, turned off the car, and sagged back into the seat. "Jeeeesus. Anyway, Kate's gay."

Ivy's hands slipped off the handle. "She's what? Oh my god. Wait, she's a cop!"

"Yep!"

"Aren't cops awful to us?"

"Cops are awful full stop," Frankie said. "Like, as an institution. Did you read that book I gave you?"

"I'm getting to it." Ivy stared thoughtfully out the windshield. "What was that thing you were talking about last week?"

"Uh. Class traitors?"

"That's it. Total class traitor." Ivy spun her skull ring around her finger. "Wow. Chief Higgins is a lesbian. How'd you know?"

"She said she used to have a friend like *we're* friends."

"That's it?"

"She said it really pointedly!"

Ivy watched a woman push a stroller in front of their car. There was no way she'd be able to hear them; still, the girls kept quiet until the woman had passed.

"What happened?"

"I don't know. She moved."

Ivy hummed again. She slid her small hand into Frankie's slippery one and squeezed. Frankie squeezed back. They were getting out of Bulldeen together. New York, New York. Just two more years.

They sat there, Frankie's sweat drying on Ivy's hands, until someone else walked past and they pulled apart.

In her secret heart of hearts, Frankie had been picturing the classic movie montage. Funky music. Posing in front of changing rooms. No—no—*definitely* not—yes!

In reality, the usual mall music blared. Posing was less fun with people around. And while Ivy found a gorgeous pastel pink gown that flared when it twirled and made Frankie forget her own name for a second, finding Frankie's dress was proving impossible.

"We have $200 left," Ivy reminded her once they exited the boutique with her dress.

"Mrgh," said Frankie.

"I can ask my parents for more!"

"Mrgh," said Frankie again, glowering at the rest of the clothing stores. There weren't many. Little Hollow was exponentially bigger than Bulldeen, but it was still a town, not a city. You could never get lost in a Little Hollow mall.

The next store was equally fruitless. And the next. Store employees brought her every black dress they had. After a while, Frankie even tried some of them on, and Ivy told her she was beautiful, and Frankie looked in the mirror and thought...*boring*. Cocktail dresses or sleek ballroom gowns, these dresses had no drama.

Ivy rested her chin on Frankie's shoulder. "We could attack it with a sewing machine."

"I'm not *that* good." Frankie did a half-hearted twirl. Even the most dramatic makeup couldn't save this dress and its poofy sleeves. She closed herself in the changing room and rested her forehead against the mirror. All this effort for...what? Staring at each other over boys' shoulders? Chatting near the punch bowl, trying to find a way to touch each other's elbows and make it look like an accident?

"Frankie? You get lost in there?"

Frankie opened her eyes. Her reflection was so close it blurred. "Why do you even want to go to Homecoming?"

Ivy paused. "It's just...what you do. Normal people."

"Well," Frankie said, and left the rest unsaid. *We're not normal people.*

"I don't know, I want...I want to get dressed up. I want to go to a dance with my person."

There were no footsteps nearby. Frankie lowered her voice anyway. "But you're not. You're going with Marvin. I'm with KJ."

"No," Ivy said. "We're going together. The boys are just our meal tickets."

Frankie snorted. The mirror fogged. She reached up and drew a tiny heart.

Almost to the front doors, Ivy linked their elbows.

"What?"

"I saw something." Ivy steered them back into the mall. Her elbow stayed in Frankie's.

"What?" she said, when Frankie gave their linked arms a pointed look. "We're two girls on a shopping trip. Anonymous. No lesbian rumors for us in Little Hollow."

"There will be if you say that loud enough," Frankie muttered. An old woman had caught the end of Ivy's sentence and was giving them the side-eye.

Frankie bared her teeth. The old woman gasped and walked faster.

Ivy laughed. "New York's going to love you," she said, dragging Frankie into a...costume shop? It was small and cramped, barely enough room for one girl per aisle, let alone two. They unlinked their arms, Ivy catching Frankie's hand to lead her up to the counter.

A man with a shockingly loud checkered shirt looked up from his book. "Yes?"

"Do you have any black dresses for my girl?" Ivy rubbed the inside of Frankie's elbow, and Frankie tried not to smile. *My girl, my girl, my girl.*

The man didn't look at their joined hands, Ivy's thumb rubbing small lines on Frankie's arm. He sniffed, jerked his head toward the back of the shop. "Follow me."

They followed, Frankie at the back, her hand in Ivy's. She watched Ivy's familiar form, all the clothes lined up around them, and imagined a deep forest where no one else could enter.

A flash at the corner of her eye. Frankie turned toward it.—

A denim-clad leg vanished behind a rack of clothes, trailing red. Cheerleader red. Blood red. Frankie snapped her head back to watch Ivy, their joined hands, this forest of clothes.

The man burped. "'Ere we go," he said, coming to a stop in front of a dusty rack of dark clothing that made synapses ping through Frankie's head. He reached in, rifling through eight different tones of black before emerging with a heavy black dress. "This one's our best. More money, but worth it."

He pushed it into Frankie's hands and stomped off.

Frankie ran her hands over the fabric. It was heavy, soft, and thick, nothing like the cheap plastic she'd seen in the rest of the shop.

Ivy raised her voice. "Where are the changing rooms?"

The man pointed without looking back. Frankie followed his finger toward a rickety stall with a ratty curtain that didn't close all the way.

"I'll stand in front," Ivy said. "Guard you from prying eyes."

Frankie looked around the empty shop. The man couldn't see them from the front desk. She shot Ivy a smile. "I wouldn't hate *some* prying eyes."

Two minutes and some tricky button work later, Frankie pulled the curtain back.

"Are you sure you don't need my help, those buttons looked..." Ivy trailed off. A flush rose in her cheeks, and Frankie didn't bother holding back her grin.

"Oh my god," Ivy said, hushed. "Baby, it's perfect."

"*Right?*" Frankie twirled, and her dress almost knocked over two clothing stands. There was nothing sheer about this dress, nothing short or smooth. It had *layers*. Silvery lace spidered along the neckline and down a single sleeve, which, upon investigation, was the only sleeve the dress had. The bright lace only made the dress look even darker, its many folds dissolving into each other. It was the kind of dress you wore while carrying a candle through a castle at night. The kind of dress you wore while being hunted by a vampire, chased by a werewolf—

A flash of red and denim. Sharp cheekbones. Frankie stopped spinning.

Ivy traced the lace pattern down the sleeve. "This was so worth it. We'd never find anything like this in Bulldeen."

"You girls from Bulldeen?"

Frankie looked up. The man from the counter was limping toward them.

"Should've known," he said. "You got the look."

Frankie glanced at Ivy, who looked equally confused. The *look*?

The man scratched his checkered shirt. "Heard there's hope. Field's started growing back."

"*One* plant," Ivy said. "That's hardly hope."

The man shook his head. "Nah. More than that. Maybe not a field—but more."

He didn't look particularly happy about it. The back of Frankie's head itched. What did this man know? What did the surrounding towns know about Bulldeen: dark fairy tales? *A friend of a friend told me this?* Did they try to stay away? Take a different route so they didn't have to pass through the town on their way to something better?

The itch grew hooks. *Go back. You need to go back.*

"We need to go," Frankie blurted.

Ivy took it well. She paid while Frankie was getting changed so fast she started sweating again. She even remembered to grab the bag while Frankie stormed out of the store. She only asked Frankie if she was okay three times while getting to the car, and only called it quits when Frankie jerked out of the parking space and almost crashed into a minivan full of children.

"I'm fine," Frankie gasped. "It's fine."

She white-knuckled the steering wheel the whole way back to Bulldeen. Ivy put on some music, and Frankie sweated even with the windows down. No dents in the car, at least. Ivy's dad would be none the wiser.

Ivy unpeeled her hands from the grab handle. "Frankie."

"Uh-huh," Frankie croaked. The Bulldeen sign was coming up. She could taste the relief coming up her throat. Almost—

"I just—" Ivy started.

A woman stood in the road. No, not a woman—not yet. Not ever. A *girl* stood in the road, the same age Frankie was now. Her stomach was carved out, rot dripping down her legs.

April Tanner's mouth opened. A maggot wormed out her sharp, rotting cheek. A voice in Frankie's head —

Frankie screamed. The car careened sideways, Frankie pumping desperately at the breaks. The world blurred, the seatbelt cut into her chest. Finally they jerked to a stop.

Frankie heaved back into her seat, blinking spots from her eyes. They were inches from a gate post fencing in the thornfruit fields. Empty dirt stretched for miles. Frankie stared at it with a strange viciousness. *Still dead. You're still dead, the town's still dying, no matter what you do—*

Ivy's panicked breathing dragged her back. Oh shit, *Ivy.*

"Are you okay?" Frankie unbuckled Ivy's seatbelt with shaking hands. "Ivy? Babe, are you—"

Ivy sucked in a breath. "What the hell was *that?*"

"A squirrel," Frankie said.

Ivy scrubbed at her cheek. A tear had escaped. "I didn't see—"

"It was super fast," Frankie said, wiping Ivy's cheek dry

with a shaking hand. "I'm so sorry, I should've just hit it. They tell you not to swerve."

Ivy stared at her, blue eyes wide and scared and wet. Her jaw flexed. Did she believe her? Frankie couldn't tell. She squeezed her eyes shut, trying not to remember April's words spilling out wrong, like a movie with an audio track playing two seconds too late.

You know what you have to do, April had said.

chapter
eight

FRANKIE KNOCKED TWICE.

Ivy's bedroom door swung open. She was in her kitten PJs, which she only wore when she needed comfort.

Frankie waved. Held up a box of Ivy's favorite form of comfort other than her girlfriend. "Guess who's on Hock Duty today?"

Hock Duty was what townsfolk did when the baker, Mr. Hockstetter, passed out drunk in the kitchen. Which was most days. Because it was right next to the police station, this usually meant cops serving up muffins and coffee. One of the cops, Deputy Lissiter, actually added extra treats to the menu. People lined up around the block when he was behind the counter. Deputy Lissiter in an apron meant crusty pies, sweet buns, and most importantly: raspberry donuts à la Lissiter, Ivy's favorite.

Ivy held the door open. Frankie snuck in. It was Friday night, and Ivy's parents had been as begrudging as ever to see Frankie. Luckily there had been no damage to Mr. Wexler's car when they'd snuck it back into the garage.

You girls spend all day together, Mr. Wexler had said when he opened the front door. *Gonna be spending all tomorrow together, getting ready for the dance. Can't spend one night apart, huh?*

Nope, Frankie had said, walking in donut-box-first.

Their dresses hung from the doorknob of Ivy's closet, black on red. Frankie would indeed come over to get ready. And then...

Frankie shuddered.

"What?"

Frankie shook her head as she settled on the bed. "Cold."

Ivy pulled up the duvet, folding it around Frankie's shoulders. "Gimme that box."

Frankie pulled it open. Four donuts sat at the bottom, gleaming pink.

"How did they still have any left?"

Frankie shrugged. "Lissiter does orders if you pay him extra. I picked these up. I...I want to make a joke about policemen and donuts but I can't think of any. Pretend I said something good."

Ivy twisted her mouth, trying to keep the smile under control. She had bags under her eyes. She insisted she was sleeping alright, but she still yawned in class. She wasn't falling asleep in class like Frankie—or in the resulting detention, jerking awake from strange, muddled dreams where someone was singing a song that slipped from her fingers between one blink and the next; the teacher staring at the unexplainable tears flowing down her cheeks—but she still yawned in class, although without actually falling asleep. Frankie, on the other hand, would find herself jerking awake during a lesson, or the resulting detention, emerging from strange, muddled dreams where someone was singing a song that slipped from her focus between one blink and the next, the teacher staring at the unexplainable tears.

Still, Ivy was definitely tired. The one time Frankie had

dared to ask about Ivy's dreams, Ivy had claimed they were normal. Frankie said, "Yeah, me too." Ivy looked disappointed, but denied it.

Ivy took a donut from the box. "Thank you," she said quietly, and chewed.

Their knees bumped. They munched on donuts. It could have been a comfortable silence, if not for the dead sister and the dreams and the secrets and the screams.

Frankie was a fast eater. She finished her two by the time Ivy reached in for her second.

She unstuck her second donut and frowned. "What's..."

She trailed off. At the bottom of the box, in glittering red and black marker, was a question:

Homecoming?

"I said I'd make you a sign," Frankie said. "I know the night before is cutting it close, but still."

Ivy wiped icing off the *O*. "Did Lissiter see?"

"Yeah, 'cause I'm an idiot. No, I took the donuts out and wrote the sign then put them back in."

Ivy stared into the donut box. Pink icing gleamed at the end of her finger and the corner of her mouth, where before the scab had been.

Frankie twisted her rings. "I...I know we went to all that trouble getting dates, and the dresses are paid for, and we didn't keep the receipts, but you're being silent a *little* too—"

Ivy kissed her, muffling Frankie's words against her mouth. When she pulled back her eyes were bright, and for a second Frankie forgot the darkness looming ahead.

"Yes," Ivy gasped. "A thousand times yes. I got asked to Homecoming in freshman year, before Marvin, and I spent the whole proposal just—like, the guy was nice! And sweet, and everything a girl should want in a boyfriend. And my smile felt so stupid, and my excitement was so fake, and I was *sure* someone would call me out on it. But no one did. And I just... told myself I was happy about it."

She kissed icing off Frankie's thumb. "It's nice. To be actually happy about it."

Frankie swallowed around a thick throat. Behind Ivy, the dresses lay against each other, waiting to be filled. They couldn't have it all, arms around each other and swaying under the disco ball. But they could have some of it, if they were careful.

Ivy covered her mouth. Frankie was touched until she recognized the noise behind her hand.

"Was that a burp? Did you sully our big romantic moment with a *burp*?"

"Shut up!" Ivy hid her face in Frankie's shoulder. "I just had dinner! Halfsies?"

She held out the donut. Frankie unsheathed her knife and flipped it open.

"This was the first thing I ever did with this knife," she said as she cut a careful line down the donut. "I mean, close enough. I cut a croissant in half."

"April said the first thing you did was cut your thumb when you tried to flip it."

The blade stopped. The donut was cleaved, blade resting gently against Ivy's palm underneath.

"When—?"

"We saw you flipping it in the parking lot," Ivy said hurriedly. "I remember—everyone was surprised. Sometimes we forgot you were sisters. She was even smiling, watching you flip that knife."

Frankie looked away.

Ivy grabbed her hand. "Not in a bad way! In a *I love my*

stupid sister kind of way."

She rubbed Frankie's hand, smearing icing. The donuts were messy, the icing just as sticky as the crimson filling. Once, April had walked in on Frankie eating one, had seen the filling dripping down her lap, and asked if she had shot herself.

Ivy reached over and plucked tissues from the nightstand, wiping their fingers clean, then the dots on their legs.

"I'm sorry," Frankie said as Ivy dabbed at her tights. "We never talk about it. She was your friend, too."

Ivy's dabbing paused. "Not really. She was someone I sat with at lunch. Opposite ends of the table. She didn't sit next to freshmen."

Frankie groaned. "Ugh. She was a *sophomore*. There's barely a difference!"

"I know!" Ivy crumpled the tissues, looking surprised and pleased at Frankie's tone. In the rare times when they veered close to the subject of April, Frankie steered them away as fast as possible.

Ivy touched the holes in Frankie's tights, nail holes caused at Kate's house. "New fashion statement?"

"You know it." Frankie pulled a hole bigger, thigh to knee.

"Cut that out." Ivy held her hand, and Frankie was reminded of every time Frankie had stopped Ivy from picking at her skin.

The box rested on the bed. Ivy picked it up, smiling softly at the glittery question. "And everyone says you aren't sweet."

"I'm not. And if you tell anyone otherwise..." Frankie held up the knife, clad with icing.

Ivy giggled, leaning forward. She dragged her tongue up the flat of the blade.

"Careful."

Ivy licked the razor tip. "You won't let me cut myself."

"Not how licking a knife works," Frankie mumbled, a flush

rising in her cheeks.

Ivy's tongue stayed against the knife. No pressure, just resting. It was a very satisfying pink. Had Frankie ever told her that? It sounded like the sort of stupid thing she'd say when she was drunk on kisses.

Ivy smiled around the blade. Her eyes glinted, wide and dark. There was something hopeful underneath the heat, an unspoken plea that had risen many times during the first few months of their relationship. *Can we just forget about everything that's going on and just—?*

Frankie dropped the knife and kissed her. Ivy's hands came up to frame her face. Her grip was hard, almost desperate. She tasted like berries and bitterness, an acrid taste under her tongue that made Frankie think of smoke. *Not smoke*, Frankie berated herself. *Jesus shit, just let us have this.*

Ivy pushed her down on the bed and stared. Her hair fell around Frankie, a dark forest with light ends. How many times had the world narrowed into that forest? Frankie touched the pale ends, twisting a strand around her finger.

Ivy watched the movement, already breathing faster. Frankie saw something else behind her eyes. Not hope or heat. Guilt?

Ivy bent down.

Ask your girlfriend what her first plan was.

Frankie wet her lips. "Sugarsnap."

"Babe?"

She was so close. Frankie could feel her breath on her mouth. "Your first plan...it was always to ask the freaky goth girl for Babylove help, right? You didn't think about anyone else?"

Ivy's playful smile twitched. "No," she said, and the line she stroked against Frankie's cheek was so gentle Frankie almost believed her. "It was always you."

chapter
nine

FRANKIE SPUN half-heartedly in Ivy's bedroom. The dress
flared out. It was even more beautiful away from the dim light
of the costume shop. Frankie tried to claw back that awed
excitement she'd felt the first time she'd tried it, but all she
could muster was a vague acknowledgement. The dress was a
goth's dream. Big whoop. All Frankie wanted to do was
collapse into bed and sleep, dreamless and lovely. Instead, she
was going to make small talk with some guy in their crappy
school gym and pretend not to be in love with her girlfriend.

An itch at the back of her head. *Something awful is going to
happen something awful has happened something awful is going
to happen again—*

A small hand touched the nape of her neck. Frankie
jumped.

"Sorry," Ivy said, appearing at her side in the mirror. "I
have a surprise."

"Good surprise?"

"No, I'm Carrie-ing you." Ivy laughed. "Close your eyes
and lift your hair out of the way."

Something thin and soft slipped around her neck.

"Okay...open!"

Frankie's eyes fluttered open. Looking in the mirror, she felt her lips part, a gasp falling from them before she could stop it.

It was a ribbon, deep red, almost the same shade as Ivy's dress. A neat bow sat at the back of Frankie's neck.

"If it doesn't suit your dress," Ivy started, and Frankie realized she'd been silent too long. "We can take it off. I just thought it'd be nice to match."

"No, I love it—" Frankie paused. "Match?"

Ivy bared her neck, revealing a thin strip of black lace. "Like it?"

"I love it," Frankie croaked. She fitted her pinkie finger in between the lace and skin, tugging gently, afraid to break it. She spun back to the mirror, drinking in their reflections. "I—this looks so cool, oh my *god*."

The enthusiasm was mostly real. She still couldn't conjure that awestruck feeling about the dress. But she was always thrilled by Ivy.

She took Ivy's hands, rubbing the skull ring on Ivy's finger that used to belong to her. "Dance with me."

"Now?"

"Before the boys get here. We can't do it at the dance, so..." She pulled Ivy close. Ivy was in heels, but Frankie was in her tallest boots, so the added height evened out.

Frankie slid her arms around Ivy's waist, turning her face into Ivy's hair, which was an elegant pile on top of her head. She'd gotten Frankie to help. Frankie nosed along a braid she'd folded into place along Ivy's hairline, wishing they could stay here all night, hidden away in the depths of Ivy's room. Nothing could get to them here. No judging stares, no bad music, no whispers of *lesbigays* from judging classmates. Surely if they stayed long enough there would be no horrifying dread spelling out guilt and doom—

"Marvin said they're going to kick you off the cheerleading team," Frankie said in a rush.

Ivy pulled back. She hesitated. "Not...yet."

"Not yet? You knew?"

Ivy shook her head. Not a no—a dismissal. *Let's not talk about this now.*

"It's all worth it," she whispered. "I'm happy with you. I was never happy with them, I was just pretending. You're the only real thing in my life."

She smiled. It looked so close to genuine Frankie could almost ignore the worry behind it. She opened her mouth—

"Ivy! Francesca! Your dates are here!"

Ivy groaned. "Here we go. Kiss for strength?"

Ignoring the dread building in her stomach, Frankie kissed her. Then they reapplied each other's lipstick.

The Wexlers insisted Ivy and Marvin pose for photos. Frankie went to stand in the hallway. KJ followed, hands in his pockets. It turned out he did own a tux, albeit baggy and moth-eaten.

After several awkward minutes of watching the photo-taking session, KJ turned to her.

"You look great."

Frankie gave him the driest look she could manage.

"No, you're right," he said. "Stupid of me. I meant you look like dogshit."

A startled snort escaped Frankie's mouth. She couldn't remember the last time a boy made her laugh. It didn't last long, the dread still swarming.

He gave her a strange look.

"What?"

"I don't know. Do you ever get the feeling..." He trailed off. A flicker of fear, almost impossible to catch. Then it was gone.

He shrugged, shoulders shifting in his baggy jacket. "The music is going to be awful."

"You know it," Frankie mumbled. She had no idea what music he listened to.

Ivy appeared in the hall, flustered and gorgeous and pulling at Frankie to leave. Her parents waved them goodbye from the door, and Frankie waved back despite Ivy's questioning look. She couldn't help it—she liked Ivy's parents sometimes. Even if they were only taking pictures to prove how perfect their daughter was, their daughter who they knew nothing about, they were still *there*, waving until the car drove out of sight.

Frankie glared daggers into the back of Marvin's head for the whole ride to school. Dread was difficult. Dread made her gut churn. *Hate* was easy, and hating Marvin had only gotten easier since Ivy. It helped that he was such a shitty driver, his Volvo jerking to a stop in the school parking lot so hard everybody slammed against their seatbelts.

"Nice one," KJ choked, rubbing his throat. His seatbelt had caught him in the neck.

Marvin sprinted around the car to open Ivy's door for her. Ivy shot an exasperated glance into the backseat, and Frankie rolled her eyes in answer.

KJ looked over, amused. "Do you want me to—"

"I will slam the door in your face."

KJ nodded. "Cool."

Marvin bowed before the open passenger door. "The dance floor awaits, milady."

Milady, Ivy and Frankie mouthed in one, as Ivy was dragged out of the car.

Streamers hid the scorch marks on the gym ceiling. A disco ball hung from the ceiling, throwing light onto the walls. A fast song was playing, one of the top hits Frankie secretly hummed to when she was alone. The students of Bulldeen High shuffled and krumped, a few trying ineffectually to slow dance.

"Three songs," Marvin reminded Ivy. "You promised."

He held out a hand. Ivy took it.

"I'll come find you after," she whispered to Frankie, and then she was tugged onto the dance floor.

Frankie watched them go. KJ sniffed, his elbow far too close for Frankie's liking.

"Wanna—?"

"I don't want to dance," Frankie blurted.

His face didn't change. "I was going to ask if you wanted to see if the punch was spiked."

"Oh. Sure."

They headed over to the drinks table. It was covered in a plastic tablecloth, available at the Shop N' Save for ninety-nine cents. KJ took the ladle—also plastic—and poured two (plastic) cups.

Frankie took a sip and gagged.

"Oh yeah," KJ said hoarsely. "Super spiked. Whoa."

He put it down. Frankie looked at him questioningly, her cup already halfway back to her mouth.

"I don't partake," he said.

"Sure, but not in *anything*?"

"Nope."

"Okay, weirdo." Frankie skulled the rest of her cup, leaving black lipstick marks on the rim. She wiped them off with her single sleeve. She didn't know how she'd wash this dress— could it even go in the washing machine?—but fashion consequences were far down her list of priorities. Ivy was spinning slowly under the disco ball, Marvin's hands on her waist. His frosted tips were slicked back, his satisfied smile oddly soft as he gazed down at her. They looked good together, if you didn't know their history.

Frankie tore her gaze away. KJ was eyeing the ribbon around her throat.

"Got any smokes?"

They made their way wordlessly back out into the chilly September night. KJ led her around the gym, out of sight of the front doors. Frankie unsheathed a pack of cigarettes, a lighter and her pocketknife.

KJ frowned at her dress. "Deep pockets."

"I know. It's perfect," Frankie said dully, sliding the knife back into its depths.

They lit up in silence. Other than the gym spillover from around the corner, the spots of light at the ends of their cigarettes were their only source of light. No stars or moon leaked through the clouds.

Frankie shivered, thinking of locked doors. Collapsed bridges. *There is no escape.*

"So what were you doing talking to Chief Higgins?"

Frankie jumped. "What? Uh. I was asking about..."

She waved her cigarette at the gym until KJ's blank face twitched with realization.

"Right. Sorry." There was no casual way to bring up the dead sister thing.

"It's fine." Frankie sucked on her cigarette. Sweet, lung-killing nectar. She should stop, but it looked cool and calmed her down and she could never really imagine living past thirty.

"When did *you* talk to Kate?"

KJ blew out a thin stream of smoke. "After this party a few years back. I was having a really bad high."

God, Frankie wished she'd brought weed. She didn't get high much anymore, but the past few weeks had her craving that small, sweet moment right at the start of the joint where everything felt okay.

"I thought you *didn't partake.*"

"Not anymore." KJ scratched his chin. He had tracks of stubble, but they were invisible in the low light. "Anyway, she caught me, uh..."

"Tripping?"

"No." KJ didn't laugh. He took another drag, so long and slow Frankie was going to ask him to get on with it.

"I was kissing a boy."

Frankie's mouth clicked shut. She turned fully to face KJ, a slouching silhouette in the dark. He stared down at his polished shoes. For several long moments the only movement was the smoke drifting into the night.

Frankie's mind whirred. She'd known this guy her whole life. Never really talked to him, but still—he was there, in the background. Just one of the guys. She never would have suspected.

She swallowed. "I thought me and Ivy were the only ones in town."

KJ's head jerked. Just a little bit, not even enough to look at her properly. "You're not."

Laughter floated around the corner. People were still piling into the gym. Pink light seeped onto the concrete, more the suggestion of light than the reality of it. Still not enough to see each other's eyes.

Relief cut through the dread. Almost enough to smother it. She was glad he'd told her in the dark. It was better, not having to look at each other.

"Now I wish I'd gotten a nice boy for you to go with," Frankie said. "We could've swapped."

KJ made a noise. Not quite a laugh.

"Who'd you kiss?"

Another long drag. "Dude Marsh."

Frankie went cold. *Why say his last name,* she thought distantly as the dread surged back with force. *There were no other Dudes in Bulldeen. Dead Freak Dude Marsh, goddamn it—*

"I don't know what happened last year," KJ added, talking faster than she'd ever heard him. "I wasn't involved. I wasn't—"

"Dude didn't tell you anything?"

KJ shook his head.

"Nothing? Like—like how to get rid of something?"

"Rid of what? Babe?"

"No! The thing killing people."

"Was that NOT Babe?"

He's a good kid, Kate had said. Like it would've mattered. Babylove was a good cat. It didn't make any difference when he plunged his fangs into that dog's throat, that kid's arm.

"I don't think so." Frankie scratched her eye. Her nail came away black. She'd forgotten about the makeup. She stared at it, imagining the smudge growing until it ate up her hand, her arm, her heart—

She shuddered. "Something dark. Something that kept the town alive. And they killed it, so now the town's dead. *That* thing."

"Not dead," KJ said hoarsely. "We have those plants, right? They started growing. If you're—if you're right, somebody must have..."

She couldn't see KJ's expression in the disco overspill, the small glow of the cigarettes. But she could see the shape of him, suddenly still.

"Did you..." His voice lowered. Nobody would hear him, and yet—his voice lowered, the way everyone lowered their voice in Bulldeen when talking about these things. "Frankie. Did you *do* something?"

Panic took Frankie by the throat. They'd had two conversations together, all within the last week. Even with the confessions, the relief and recognition—there was no situation where Frankie would stay.

He didn't call her name as she ran away. Or maybe he did and Frankie couldn't hear it, her heartbeat too loud in her ears, drowning out the music as she stumbled around the corner and into the gym.

The disco ball spun. A shard of light cut her face. Frankie's eyes watered. Her cheeks were still wet when she spotted Ivy at the drinks table, wrinkling her nose as she resurfaced from a glass of punch.

"There you are," she said as Frankie ran up. "He finally let me go, said something about fixing his hair—"

Frankie took her wrists. "Dance with me."

Ivy's hands flexed around her cup. Light tangled in her eyelashes, making her squint. The disco ball was shockingly bright, making dancers wince whenever it found them. Some things weren't meant for direct light. Some things were meant to happen in the dark.

"We can't," Ivy said.

Frankie nodded to a corner where the light couldn't touch. "Just for a second. No one will see us."

"Frankie—"

"It's *2004*," Frankie hissed. "Britney and Madonna kissed on *live TV*! There are scarier things than two girls dancing!"

Ivy was still shaking her head, eyes full of tears, and Frankie thought back to their first kiss in Ivy's driveway: terror, dread, deep want. Ivy slid her hand out from Frankie's grip, reaching up to scratch the long-healed spot next to her mouth.

Frankie caught it. She hadn't finished saying 'Don't' when she caught a flash over Ivy's shoulder.

It wasn't movement. Everything was moving: the disco ball,

the colored lights, the dancers sliding awkwardly into each other's arms for a slow dance. The music had ticked over.

This wasn't movement: it was stillness. Horrible stillness—KJ with his cigarette, Ivy turning down a dance. There, over Ivy's unmoving shoulder, stood April Tanner. Stomach scooped out. Blood dripping down her jeans. Eyes white.

She was on the other side of the gym. Then Frankie blinked, and she was right behind Ivy.

"*Sis,*" said April, her voice like flies buzzing, animals crying, a hundred fields rotting. "*She still hasn't told you?*"

chapter
ten

FRANKIE SCREAMED.

If it happened thirty seconds later, it might have been lost in the thrum of dance music. Thirty seconds earlier and it would have been hidden under a rising piano tune. This unfortunate scream happened in the two-second gap between songs, and the gym rippled with heads turning to gawk at Loser Tanner, Tanner the freak, Tanner the recently-only-child decked out in even more black than usual, and screaming right into Ivy Wexler's face.

"What? What is it?" Ivy turned. Frankie waited for her searching gaze to rove uselessly over someone only Frankie could see—

But Ivy shrieked. She wasn't the only one. Shocked yells echoed through the gym as Ivy jerked away, stumbling into the drinks table.

"Jesus," Ivy gasped as punch slopped over the bowl, dripping down the table onto her high heels. "Is—oh god, is that *April*?"

April. Whispers through the gym, audible even as the music kicked up. Hunched shoulders, lips curled back in disgust, terrified gazes turning away whenever Frankie met them. Dancers spun to a stop. The Grisham sisters stopped mid-krump to gape in horror.

April smiled, blood pouring from the growing hole in her stomach, and vanished.

"Oh god," Ivy said. She reached a trembling hand into the suddenly empty space. "Oh my god."

Frankie grabbed Ivy's shoulders. "You saw her?"

"Just for a second," Ivy whispered, eyes wide.

The beat quickened. A lone junior stopped doing the funky chicken, turning to see why no one was joining in. Someone pointed at Frankie.

"We need—" Ivy started.

Frankie didn't let her finish, already dragging her out.

The bathroom door slammed shut. Frankie spun Ivy to face her in front of the sinks.

"Oh my god." Ivy repeated, staring at their joined hands. "Oh my god, *April*."

"What was she saying?"

"I—what?"

"What haven't you told me?"

Ivy stared at her, lost. Her blue eyes tracked nothing, catching up, trying to make sense. She hadn't heard that part. She hadn't been seeing a bloody April Tanner for weeks—it would take her a minute.

"Why is she here?" Ivy asked. "What...what..."

Frankie could feel her face doing something damning. All this time, she would have folded if Ivy asked her the right question. She watched, the dread in her gut surging through to the tips of her fingertips as Ivy realized. It came in increments: disbelief. Fear. Horror. It came in silence, the two of them clutching each other in the empty bathroom until Ivy finally asked the right question:

"What did you *do?*"

Frankie sucked in a shaky breath. The words fell out and splattered to the floor: "I just missed her so much. I just gave it my blood. I didn't finish—I didn't say the words, not all of them, I thought about Babylove and Babe. I—I couldn't do it. I *couldn't.*"

Ivy stumbled back. Her heel, slick with spiked punch, slid on the linoleum.

Frankie reached to steady her. "Hey—"

Ivy lurched back, out of reach. "Whatever the Dead Freaks did last year—you saw what happened—it killed all those people! It killed *April!*"

Something dripped down Frankie's chin. She scrubbed at it, thinking of blood, black ooze, rancid thornfruit juice, but her hand came away stained with mascara and salt.

Frankie steeled herself. "What haven't you told me, Ivy?"

The horror did not leave Ivy's face. It just transformed. Outwards to inwards. Until then, Frankie had been hoping it was a lie. A trick from the ugly parts of Bulldeen, trying to divide and conquer. But there was no mistaking the way Ivy shrank, collarbones stark against her chest as it heaved.

A short knock on the door. "Ladies?"

Frankie swiped again at her face. "Go away, KJ!"

"Got it," KJ said hastily. "Just wanted to let you know Ivy's ex is booking it over here and he's being even more charming than—"

Muffled grunting. KJ's voice floated through the door: *Jesus, whatever, go for it.*

The door swung open. Marvin strode in, frustration glitching for a moment as he registered his deep disgust at stepping foot in the women's bathroom. Then he shook his head, a tight smile worming onto his face.

"There you are," he said in the worst approximation of bright Frankie had ever heard. "Come on, the line for pictures has dried up."

He held out a manicured hand.

Ivy stared at it. "What?"

"Pictures," Marvin repeated. "We didn't do it on the way in."

"We..." Ivy pushed hair away from her forehead, dewy with sweat under the foundation. "We took pictures."

Marvin laughed. It was grating. Frankie wanted to push him into the sinks.

"Your *parents* took pictures. We need pictures at the actual dance. You know how it goes."

KJ cleared his throat. He was holding the door open with his body, still in the hall, like he wasn't fully committed unless he took a step into the room. "Man, were you even in the gym a minute ago?"

Marvin turned to look at him like he was offended KJ was even talking to him. He shook his head, less a reply and more shaking off the question.

"Come on," he repeated, hand still aloft. "The line's empty. What are you girls *doing* in here?"

Frankie slapped his hand out of the air in a deranged high-five. "Because everyone's freaked out by my dead sister, you little shit! Get out of our *faces!*"

She turned to Ivy, ignoring Marvin's confused spluttering. "We shouldn't have come. We need to go."

Marvin asked Ivy, "Is she serious?"

Ivy didn't look at him. She didn't look at Frankie. Her small hand reached up and scratched at the skin next to her mouth until it went red.

"Whoa," KJ muttered. "Here she comes."

Frankie was turning to ask *who* when Kate Higgins walked into the bathroom, sparing Marvin an annoyed look.

"Wait," KJ continued. "Someone actually called the cops?"

"I was in the area," Kate said, and jerked her head. "Boys. This is the ladies' room. *Out.*"

KJ immediately stepped further into the hall, the door swinging shut without his weight.

"But—" Marvin started.

Kate stepped close. She came up to his forehead. Was Kate short? Frankie had never noticed. She gave off impeccable vibes of being taller than whoever she talked to.

"Out," she said, teeth clicking on the T.

Marvin's teeth flashed in another tight smile. "I was just grabbing my girlfriend, if you'll just—"

Kate took him by the front of the shirt and shoved. "I said *out*, shitheel."

Marvin hit the door shoulder-first, gasping in pain. He looked at the girls in shock. When they did absolutely nothing, his face twisted.

"Fine," he spat. "But my...my parents will hear about what you just did!"

"Cry me a river," Kate intoned. The door swung shut. Kate turned to the girls, voice dropping. "Kids are saying they saw April Tanner. You know anything about this?"

Frankie snorted wetly. "You were in the area, huh?"

Kate stared her down with more intensity than Frankie thought she was capable of. "Do you *know*?"

Guilt hung thick in the air. Frankie's mind whirled with horrible things Ivy could be guilty of.

Kate sighed through her teeth. Pinched the bridge of her nose. Cigarettes and booze always made her look older than her years, but for a second Kate Higgins looked ancient, heavy under the weight of whatever Bullden had piled on top of her.

"I can remember the ritual," she said. "Anything I forget, Milly will remind me. Let's go."

"Wait," Ivy said. "What?"

Kate unsheathed her gun, clicking the chamber out to count the bullets. "We're going up to Juniper Lookout," she said, shoving the gun back into its holster. "If that place still works. Do you still have your knife?"

"Juniper *what*?" Ivy said, looking automatically at Frankie, a question that went from silent to nonexistent once she saw Frankie's face.

A knock at the door. Kate swore as Marvin's voice floated through: "Are you done? I need to talk to Ivy."

"And I need to talk to you," Frankie said to Kate, voice shockingly steady despite the tears still streaming down her face.

"Later," Kate said. "We need—"

"Do you know what Ivy's keeping from me?"

Kate's arm paused. She'd been about to shoulder the door open, regardless of who might be standing directly behind it.

"Not right now," she said.

Frankie shook her head. "You guys were talking about something at my place. What was it?"

A small hand on her single sleeve, gentle through the fabric. An hour ago Ivy had been rubbing it, admiring the sheerness. *Like a butterfly wing*, she'd said, and made Frankie twirl for her.

Now here they were: stuck in a bathroom with a cop in front of the door, an ex-boyfriend behind, fluorescent light flooding the room. It was too bright. Some conversations should happen in the dark.

"She still hasn't told you," Frankie said, and she sounded

79

nothing like her sister—in life or in death. No scraping rocks or put-on syrupy sweetness that curdled at the core. Frankie was always low bass and rough edges.

"Told me what," Frankie said.

Ivy flinched. "Frankie..."

"Told me *what?*" Frankie's voice broke. She could see herself in the mirror over Ivy's shoulder, blurry through her tears: dark streaks down her ruddy cheeks, eyeshadow rubbing off, hair a mess. The last time she'd felt this helpless, she'd been in Ivy's basement with the wind picking up. She'd hoped she had grown in the past year. Apparently not.

"Girls," Kate tried.

More knocking. Marvin pried the door open. "I really need to talk to Ivy!"

Kate jerked the door into his face. He reeled back, cursing, and only getting louder as Kate held the door shut with her foot.

Ivy took Frankie's hands. Black nail polish against red. Frankie used to think it was romantic. Only now did she think of blood and bruises.

"Before I tell you," Ivy said shakily, "I need you to know how much I love you. I'm *so* excited about New York, about our lives together."

Frankie waited. Every fiber of her wanted to say the eternal reply: *I love you too.* But the look in Ivy's eyes was so heavy it made her hesitate.

"I would do anything for you," Ivy rushed. "*Anything.* You know that, right?"

"Ivy. Just say it."

Ivy's mouth moved around open air. Her lips trembled.

"That first time you came over," she whispered. "Before I knew you, I thought I might have to... sacrifice you."

A noise punched out of Frankie's throat. Almost a laugh.

Standing there at the top of Ivy's stairs, she'd even said it: *If you brought me down here to kill me, you really should've made me walk in first.*

I'm not going to kill you, Ivy had said, too fast. It had made Frankie nervous. She'd brushed it off later, a nervous assurance between two girls who didn't trust each other yet. Only now did she remember the stark whites of Ivy's eyes, the tremor in her voice.

Frankie felt pressure on her arms. Ivy was squeezing. "Baby—"

Frankie scoffed. "No, it makes sense. No one would miss Loser Tanner, right?"

"I knew I couldn't do it the first time we had an actual conversation! After you helped me get Babylove back in the cage, I knew—"

"That you couldn't kill me? Holy shit, *thanks.* So glad I meet the standard for Do Not Murder—"

"I'd do anything for you," Ivy cried.

Frankie twisted out of her grip. "You have...you have *no* right to be mad at me for doing the bare minimum to see my sister again. After what you did? *Oooh, Frankie, what did you do?* You *hypocrite.*"

Kate's voice rose over the yelling. "Girls!"

"*What,*" Frankie barked.

Kate pointed. The girls turned.

There, in the corner of the bathroom, April Tanner smiled. Blood poured from the gaping maw punched through her stomach. Blood dripped down her halterneck, from behind her teeth, her eyes.

Frankie heard herself say, "Holy god fucking shit Christ Jesus save us fuck."

The door slammed open. Kate stumbled, head connecting with the wall with a dull *thwack.* Marvin charged in, his back to the dead girl in the corner, trembling with righteous anger.

"I *knew* it," he hissed at Frankie. "What did you do to Ivy? Did you drag her into this, or did you do something to her?"

His hands twitched at his sides. Clean, shapely nails. Thick fingers. Frankie was all too aware how they felt around her wrists. She wasn't interested in having them wrapped around her throat.

"I didn't do anything," she said. "Marvin, you need to turn around—"

Marvin's eyes were bright, his jaw clenched. "She'd never be with you if you didn't—if you didn't do something. Blackmail, or—or some freaky goth magic!"

Kate groaned from the floor, holding her head. "For god's sake—"

Marvin surged forward. Frankie tried to step in front of Ivy; Ivy tried to step in front of Frankie. Frankie was faster.

Marvin's chest hit hers. He spared her a hateful glance before craning his head behind her. "I'll get you out of this, Ives. I promise. Whatever she's done to you—"

"Oh my GOD," Ivy said, her back against the mirror, stuck between Frankie and a hard place. "She hasn't done anything to me! Get out of here!"

April took a step out of the corner. Blood pooled on the floor, gliding ever closer. It coated Kate's leg, her hand braced on the floor. She tried crawling away from it, but the blood was coming too fast. She'd hit her head hard.

It's going to reach us, Frankie thought as Marvin crowded them into the mirror, trying to reach Ivy. *It's going to climb up our dresses and then—*

"Get the hell away from her," Marvin snarled, still oblivious.

He pinned her into the glass, Ivy trapped behind them.

Frankie tore her gaze away from the blood on the floor. "Marvin, turn the hell around."

"What did you do," Marvin said, voice breaking. A tear plunged down his cheek. "What did you *do* to her, she was normal, she was *mine*—"

"Marvin," Frankie said. "This is bigger than us, you need to turn the FUCK around—look in the goddamn mirror!"

April took another slow step, her bare feet sinking into the inch of blood coating the floor.

"Don't," Frankie said, and she didn't know who she was speaking to anymore. "Please don't..."

Blood approached the heel of Marvin's polished boots, the floor almost swallowed now. Frankie shoved, but her hands were trapped between their bodies. He was too strong.

"I'm gonna save her from you," Marvin said, staring hard into Frankie's face, pressing the girls harder into the mirror. "Hear me, you freak? I'm gonna—"

Glass cracked behind Ivy's head. Marvin looked up at all those spreading fractures. His face went slack. The mirror had become a tangled mess of sections, and April's bloody face stretched across every one.

"Oh god," Marvin said, his voice strangely blank. The horror hadn't caught up with him yet.

April grinned. Her teeth flashed across the mirror, seeping into every fissure.

Marvin's unforgiving press lessened. Not enough for Frankie to wrest her wrists free, but enough for Ivy to slip out from behind her.

"Get the fuck away from her," Ivy snarled, and shoved him sideways.

Marvin slipped on the blood-wet floor. His hit the sink with a wet *crack*. A chunk of porcelain broke off and shattered on the ground. Marvin followed, slamming into the sticky linoleum. He lay there, blood seeping into his clothes, eyes bulging bigger and bigger, trying and failing to turn his head far enough to look at the approaching April.

Blood seeped into his open mouth. He gagged. His hand came beneath him to push himself up. He managed two trembling inches, then he fell back to the floor.

"Oh god," Frankie heard someone say. "Oh god." Even later, she wouldn't know if it was her or Ivy.

The sink had caved his head in. Pink meat glistened beneath the exposed skullcap, a massive dent just beyond his hairline.

Kate fumbled for her gun. Her fingers were slow, clumsy. Head wounds made everything fuzzy.

A moan juddered from Marvin's throat. His legs jerked, then went still. His arm scrabbled ineffectively. His body was shutting down, Frankie realized numbly.

April knelt beside him. She bent over his open head.

Sacrifice, Frankie thought, and the voice almost sounded like her own.

April paused long enough to shoot the girls another grin. Nightmarish. Playful. A little bitchy. April Tanner stretched in a funhouse mirror into uncanny and terrible forms.

"It's good to see you again," she told Ivy.

The grin twitched. Sagged.

"I'mmmm... s-sorry," she said, strangely slurred, like she only had control of half of her tongue. Then she jerked back and sank her teeth into Marvin's scalp.

Marvin didn't have enough life left in him to scream. He let out another guttural, sobbing moan as April's red mouth closed around the exposed meat beneath his skull. The horrible sucking, chewing noises would haunt Frankie for the rest of her days.

Marvin went still.

Click.

Frankie barely had time to register the sound before a gunshot rang out. April jerked, blood arcing over the mirrors. She let out a high-pitched whine that was already turning into a growl as she turned toward the shooter.

Kate panted on the floor, looking up at the girls with bloodshot eyes.

"Run."

chapter
eleven

"HEY GUYS, I don't wanna get involved but I heard something. *Please* say it wasn't a gunshot—"

KJ jumped back as the bathroom door swung open, blood and girls spilling out.

"Move!" Frankie barked at him as they barrelled down the hallway.

Dancers still spun half-heartedly in the middle of the gym. You had to hand it to Bulldeen: they carried on, murder and dark magic notwithstanding. But they started clearing out pretty fast when Loser Tanner and her Close Gal Pal ran out making bloody footprints, and with the chief of police yelling at them to get the hell out, right *now*.

"Emergency exit, go go *go!*" Kate yelled, stumbling to the door and swinging it open. An alarm blared as students piled out into the parking lot. They'd installed this door halfway through the rebuild. Nothing like a gaggle of teenagers trapped in a burning gym to inspire safety procedures.

Frankie blundered toward it. Her bloody boot caught on her hem and she skidded, pitching forward.

There was a second when Frankie was so disconnected from her own body, unmoored and numb and shaking, that she nearly let herself fall. Then Ivy's arm locked around hers, the familiar weight of it sinking deep into Frankie's bones, snapping her back into focus.

"Thanks," she said.

Ivy nodded jerkily. "I got you."

"Girls!" Kate motioned for them to join the students streaming out of the exit. "Get out of here!"

A scream rang out over the upbeat music. KJ was on the floor, April's hand a manacle around his ankle, dragging him back into the hallway.

For a single, terror-drunk moment, Frankie considered the emergency exit. Other students had noticed a bloody April and were screaming too, pushing harder for the door. If you saw something horrible in Bulldeen, you turned away. Crossed the street. You ran and you didn't look back.

There were few exceptions. One of them had been April Tanner. She had stripped off her shirt to beat out the inferno on her classmate's body. It was useless, and it killed her. But she had tried.

The thing that was once April Tanner disappeared into the bathroom, movements jerky and odd, like the frame rate had been turned down. Like something was fighting from the inside, trying to stop each footstep.

Frankie ran for the hallway, Ivy falling into step at her side. Frankie pulled out her pocketknife. Ivy bent down and shucked her bloodstained high heels, holding one aloft.

KJ clung to the bathroom door frame, free leg flailing wildly. "SHIT SHIT SHIT SHIT SHIT," he yelled, trying to kick her off. "SHE'S EATING ME! HELP—"

"Shut up," Frankie told him, stepping into the blood.

April's mouth was attached to KJ's ankle. A gory bite mark showed between his baggy tuxedo pants and shiny boots, his black socks pushed down for easy access.

"Let go of him," Ivy snarled.

April's head came up a second too late, her smile coming in fitful spasms. Tears on her cheeks cut into the red around her mouth.

Frankie's heart twisted in her chest. "If you're in there, sis, I'm sorry."

She stabbed April in the hand. April reared back, grip loosening enough for Frankie and Ivy to yank KJ's leg free. KJ stumbled to his feet, falling over twice in his haste to get out of the bathroom.

"Thanks!" he screamed back as he limped desperately down the hall.

April hissed. Ivy threw her high heel. The stiletto pierced April's cheek, and Frankie heard herself let out a horrified laugh—the Tanners had always joked about cutting people with their cheekbones. Now here was that sharp cheekbone shattered with a shoe.

They ran. April's heavy, jolting footsteps pursued. Light scraped their wet faces, the disco ball spinning faster and faster. Nobody had thought to turn the lights off, and the music was playing a party song. *Die die die, baby! Everybody put your hands up!*

The last of the students fled through the emergency exit, KJ limping with them.

Kate unsheathed her gun. "Move."

Frankie and Ivy ducked sideways.

BANG-BANG.

April thudded to the floor, two bullet holes in her head, another in her cheek from the heel. Still, she writhed.

"How do we stop it?" Ivy panted. "You said Juniper —something?"

Kate checked her chamber. Two bullets left. "I don't know, Milly said—" She swiped at the back of her head. Her hair was matted with blood. "Last time I talked to her, she said this feels different. What we did to it last year, combined with the bad evocation you did—this thing isn't full strength. It needed something to help it along."

She pointed the gun at the thing that was once April Tanner, who was pushing herself up slowly, painfully, from the polished wood.

"Which means *some* of it is April. If we make it become April, then put her down, whatever's pulling her strings doesn't have anything to hold on to. Slides right back to wherever it came from."

"Put her down," Frankie repeated, reeling. She'd only understood half of what Kate was saying. "You mean—"

"She's already dead." Kate raised her gun, then paused. "Hey. Look at me. She. Is. *Dead*. She died a year ago in this goddamn gym. This is just an echo."

The creature on the floor rumbled, low in its throat. April Tanner's eyes. April Tanner's razorblade cheeks. April Tanner's sorrow, coming through in flickers only, staring at her little sister like she desperately wanted to say something, but couldn't.

Frankie felt a touch on her forehead. Ivy pushed sweaty strands out from Frankie's face, tucking them behind one ear.

"Baby," she said softly. "You should stand back."

Her smile was grim and shaking. Frankie could already see it: she'd killed Marvin. She could kill Frankie's sister, too.

Frankie felt her head shake, a slow side-to-side.

Kate sighed, gun raised. "Kid—"

"One second," Frankie croaked. "I just...I need..."

She took a step forward. April growled. Her hand swept uselessly through the air before Frankie's boot. Even numb with grief, Frankie hadn't come too close.

"Um," Frankie said. She'd had so many things she wanted

to say. How many times had she lay in bed imagining one last meeting? Now here her sister was—a trembling bloody heap trying to swipe at her, sure. But still here.

Frankie swallowed. "My grades are good. Not great, but I'm on track to pass. Get into college, even. I finally started using boot polish, you were right, it makes a big difference. And..."

She reached back, not bothering to look. Ivy's fingers slid home.

"I have somebody," Frankie said. "I love her. We're in love."

April's eyes flickered. Hate, hunger, curiosity. A small shred of happiness.

Her skull clicked back into place, skin crawling to cover it. April's mouth opened. Her tongue was clumsy, her mouth even worse. It took several tries before Frankie heard it properly:

"Shhhh...eee... good t'you?"

"She's good. We're good." Frankie's knuckles hurt with how hard Ivy was squeezing, and she'd never been more grateful for the pressure. "We're going to New York after we graduate."

"That's... nnnnice." April convulsed. She jerked forward, as if to lunge for their ankles, before slamming back into the wood. April Tanner, holding the monster at bay.

Her eyes slitted open, watering with concentration. *"I'mmm... ssssorry I was such a bitch.... T'you."*

"It's okay," Frankie whispered. Not quite the truth, but April was still talking.

"High school was aw...aw...awful. I was awful. Didn't wanna get the awful... on you." A high whine tore out of her throat, head twisting back, shoulder blades pressing hard on her skin, as if they were trying to break free. Her jaw lurched to

the side, slurring the words even further: *"Sis... can't hold this off. You gotta do it."*

Frankie felt her head shake.

"Gotta," April repeated. Her eyes flickered. *"Getting stronger. Gotta."*

"No," Frankie said, the word barely audible over the sob.

April growled and swiped. Frankie wobbled back.

Ivy said, "I'll do it."

Frankie looked at her. Ivy was crying again, but her gaze was determined.

The growl turned to a shriek. April staggered to her feet, lurching forward.

"Don't," Kate warned, shouldering in front of the girls. She raised the gun—

April ran at Kate, throwing her sideways. Shots rang out and a bullet dug into the floor, another into the scorch marks on the ceiling. Kate slammed into the wall and landed with a pained cry, leg twisted unnaturally beneath her.

April turned to the girls. She smiled. No tears down her cheeks.

Frankie held out her knife. "Don't come any closer."

April laughed like her vocal cords lived in a faraway world none of them wanted to visit. *"You won't kill me. I'm the only way you get your sister back."*

"I'm not getting her back. I think...I think I could have. But I screwed it up. And you'd be too weak to do it, anyway. Right?"

April's head tilted. She looked amused, but more than anything she looked hungry.

"Right?" Frankie glanced around for something, *anything* —Kate was prone on the floor, out of bullets. Ivy was barefoot, one high heel in the bathroom, the other on the other side of the gym. Even together, they couldn't stand against this monster in a fistfight. So all they had was this: Frankie's shitty little pocketknife that she didn't sharpen as much as she should.

Frankie glanced at Ivy. "Get behind me."

Ivy gave her an annoyed look. "What? *You* get behind *me.*"

April laughed again, plodding forward.

"I'm the one with the knife," Frankie hissed. "Get—"

"HEY ASSHOLE!"

Everyone turned. KJ stood in the gym doorway, holding a clear glass bottle with a pocket square stuffed down its neck. His other hand white-knuckled a lighter.

He sagged against the doorframe. He flicked the lighter on, pocket square catching the flame.

April's head tilted further, her smile fading.

"I found the guy who was spiking the punch," KJ said, and threw.

The bottle spun through the air, catching the light: silver and pink and purple. It was beautiful.

Then it landed on April, and that beautiful light turned explosive red. April shrieked, shards of glass embedding in her face, flames charring her skin, eating her hair.

"God," Frankie whispered. April hadn't burned to death, but her body had lain in those flames for several minutes before the rescue crew dragged her out. One side of her body, people said, was completely charred. Frankie never saw it. They did a closed casket.

The thing that looked like April roared, staggering forward. Flames flecked the floorboards, then took root.

Frankie got in front of Ivy.

"Frankie," Ivy snapped.

April's stagger turned to a run, the run to a sprint.

"Remember what Kate said—"

Frankie held up her knife.

Ivy continued, "It has to be April first."

"Wh—" The word was cut off as Ivy's small hands shoved Frankie sideways. She hit the floor in time to see Ivy bracing her bare feet, teeth bared.

April *leapt*. Ivy slammed into the ground, forearms locked over her face and neck, holding back against the snarling, charred thing on top of her. April bit a chunk out of Ivy's arm. The scream that wrenched out of Ivy's throat was worse than Marvin's death rattles, worse than the officer telling Frankie that April was dead, worse than every slammed door from her parents.

Frankie crawled, clumsy and numb, over to April's twisting body. Raised her knife. Brought it down in the middle of April's back.

April growled. Tore another knot of flesh out of Ivy's arm. Ivy screamed again.

Frankie yanked the knife out. Brought it down again, this time in April's neck. April gurgled something that might have been a laugh, Ivy's flesh stringy between her teeth.

"It's okay," Frankie screamed. "Ivy? Hear me, sugarsnap?"

Ivy looked at her through the cage of April's grip, tears and blood in her lashes. Behind them, flames grew. Smoke drifted toward the disco ball, shot through with colored lights.

Another useless stab. And another. April's back was a bloody mess, and it meant nothing. *It has to be April first.*

"I got you," Frankie told Ivy, and bent low over April's ear. Horrible, wet chewing.

Frankie shuddered. "You were right. The kindness killed you."

April hesitated mid-chew. Beneath her, Ivy whimpered. Her gaze never faltered on Frankie's, tears still streaming down her face onto the gym floorboards.

"You were always so cynical," Frankie choked. "God, you

were such a bitch. But there was something in you, deep down, that wanted to be kind."

April's head twitched. *It's the kindness that kills you.* Their mother had said it so many times. A guiding light, a warning. April had tried so hard to buy into it, just like Frankie had, and they'd both failed miserably.

Frankie reached around April with a shaking hand, angling the knife toward her chest.

"And I love you for that." Frankie choked, still watching Ivy's eyes, full of pained tears. "I want you to know. I love you so much."

April twitched, like a spider infested with a parasite, trying to regain control. A puppet taking its strings in hand. Her grip on Ivy went limp. She gave a low, wet laugh.

"Yyy...you're such a... looooser," said April Tanner, with all the scorn and love only a big sister could access. *"Frankie—"*

Frankie stabbed her through the heart.

April gasped. It was soft, almost silent. Her arms trembled, then gave way.

Ivy shoved her off, staggering to her feet. Frankie stared at the charred body lying on the floorboards. Her ears were ringing. When did that start?

She reached out and touched April's back, still riddled with wounds. April didn't move. Frankie pressed harder.

"—kie. Frankie! *Frankie!*"

Frankie startled. Ivy was staring at her, tears still streaming down her cheeks, shaking like a leaf.

Frankie staggered up and gathered Ivy into her arms, kissing her forehead, checking the bite wounds. "Are you okay? Shit, these look bad..."

Ivy winced as Frankie carefully angled her arm. Jagged scoops were missing, one on the inside of her elbow and another further up, near her shoulder. They would scar, and badly.

"I'm okay," Ivy said. "I'm—oh."

They turned to watch as April, bit by bit, became ash. First her legs and arms, the rest of her thumping into the floor with nothing to hold her up. Then her torso, her jaw, her sharp Tanner cheekbones, all of her consumed into a gray pile. From the ash rose a single thornfruit, which rotted, then turned back into ash and joined the heap.

Fire climbed the gym walls. A slow song played over the speakers.

"You girls alright?"

Frankie turned. KJ was trying to help Kate up from the floor. It was hard going—KJ had a badly bleeding ankle and Kate had what looked like a broken leg, if that awkward jut against the inside of Kate's pants was anything to go by.

Frankie had to clear her throat twice before she could speak. "We're okay."

KJ nodded, then tilted his head. "I hear sirens."

He and Kate made their way slowly, painfully, to the exit.

Ivy touched the skin below her injured elbow. "I've never been in this much pain," she said, almost dazed. "It's like...fire. Like it got me."

She looked up, where a line of flames had almost reached the ceiling. Not even one wall had been consumed yet. But there was time.

Frankie cupped her face. "You're okay. We'll get you to a hospital."

"It doesn't hurt much," Ivy said, dazed. "I think the adrenaline..."

Frankie twisted her arms carefully, looking for scorch marks. "Are you burned? Did April—"

"No, she wasn't, like, on fire. Just very hot." Ivy giggled. "I just called your dead sister hot."

Frankie couldn't help herself from glancing back at the heap of ash that was once her sister. She shuddered. "Okay. *Okay.* Let's—"

Ivy's chin wobbled. "I'm so sorry I didn't tell you about the...sacrifice thing. I should've—"

"Hey, it's okay. I didn't tell you I tried raising my sister from the dead."

The sirens were getting louder. Frankie turned to the door, where KJ was helping Kate into the parking lot. She followed, careful not to stand on Ivy's bare feet.

Silver light swept over them. Frankie stopped.

Ivy asked, "What?"

Frankie shook her head. "Nothing. I wanted...it's nothing."

Ivy looked up. They were underneath the disco ball. The doorway was empty. They were alone in the gym.

Frankie started forward.

Ivy pulled her back. "Dance with me."

Fire brushed the ceiling. The slow song continued, all soft piano and violins.

Frankie blinked. "What?"

"We've got time," Ivy said, blue eyes glinting silver in the disco light. She hooked her pinkie finger under the black ribbon on Frankie's throat.

Frankie swallowed, throat riding against Ivy's finger. "You're hurt."

"We've got time," Ivy repeated, and smiled. Her fingers were soft and shaking. As always, they fit perfectly between Frankie's.

They put their arms around each other. Ivy lay her head on Frankie's shoulder. The slow song was still playing, though that wouldn't last long. For the second time in two years, fire was eating the speaker wires.

Smoke gathered high above their heads. Flames found the disco ball, plastic motes drifting gently down around their dresses in a burning silver snowfall.

Frankie closed her eyes, pressing her face into Ivy's hair. The lavender scent was still there, buried under ash and blood.

They had under a minute before the smoke forced them out. But for that minute there were two girls in an empty gym, swaying gently under a burning disco ball as the music dripped to a stop.

chapter
twelve

TWO DAYS LATER, Frankie stepped through the sliding doors of the hospital.

Ivy squinted up at the direction signs, which were the same level of faded as when they were here yesterday. "I can't believe you've never broken a bone. Or, like, got mono. *Everybody* got mono that winter in middle school."

"I wasn't kissing anyone in middle school," Frankie reminded her. "Why, were you?"

Ivy winked. A passing nurse glanced at them. This nurse lived in Bulldeen, like a good third of the people who worked here.

Frankie watched the nurse fight against a double take: cheerleader and goth with each other's colors tied around their necks. They had decided on Homecoming night to keep the ribbons, Frankie sitting next to Ivy while she got patched up. She'd kept a hold on Ivy's hand the whole time. The doctor stared pointedly, but didn't say anything. Not even to Ivy's parents, who had both cried to see their daughter's perfect arm ruined.

Before they'd dropped Frankie off today, Mrs. Wexler had met Frankie's eyes in the rear-view mirror.

I'm glad she has a friend like you, she'd said, lips tight. *I can't imagine any of her old friends would've been as...dedicated.*

No, Frankie had replied, her hand tightening around Ivy's. *They wouldn't.*

Ivy waved at the nurse side-eyeing them. "Hi! Do you know where I could find Chief Higgins?"

The nurse's gaze lingered again on their necks, black lace and red ribbon. "Floor four, room fourteen."

She adjusted her collar, exposing a nametag: Katherine Marsh. This was Dude Marsh's mother. Dude, the Dead Freak who kissed KJ, Dude who resurrected Babe, Dude who had done god knows what last year to the people who went missing. Dude who, in all likelihood, had been there when April died. What did Katherine Marsh know about what her son had been through? If she was anything like Frankie and Ivy's parents: not much.

Frankie cleared her throat. "Thank you."

"'S what I'm here for," said Katherine Marsh, some of her son's aloofness emerging. She strode off with the quickening pace of a Bulldeen local who had just been met with the possibility of answers and wanted to get away from them as fast as humanly possible.

The elevator was clunky and slow. Frankie leaned her head on Ivy's shoulder. "Tell me about mono."

"It was tiring," Ivy told her. "It was just really tiring. I couldn't do anything. It felt like I was dead."

The elevator clunked into place. The doors slid open onto another hallway that stank of antiseptic. Frankie could smell it even under the stench of smoke that still clung to her and Ivy's hair after two days and too many showers.

A voice drifted from room fourteen. It didn't sound like any of the Higgenses. Ivy and Frankie frowned at each other.

Since when did Kate have someone other than a relative who would visit her in the hospital?

"—think you should consider a plane," a woman said as the girls entered.

Kate snorted. A book rested on her stomach. "Milly. Are *you* considering a plane?"

"No, but—"

"I'm not getting on one of those death traps."

"You can't drive to LA with a broken foot," Milly Hart argued.

Her hair was clean, and shorter than Frankie had ever seen it. She'd only talked to Milly once, last year, when all the Babylove stuff was going down. Milly was the only other person who got weird, dark books out from the library. Apparently, the Dead Freaks actually got her to talk to them about it.

"You—oh!" Milly flinched in her chair. "Hi. Hello."

"Hi hello," Frankie mimicked, not unkindly. Milly's gray eyes flickered between them, shoulders hunching. Not sure if she was being teased.

"Sorry," Frankie said.

"It was a joke," Ivy added. "How are you, Milly?"

Milly blinked. She'd have to be twenty now, Frankie guessed. Some people never aged out of being terrified of teenage girls.

"Good," she said, and stood. "I'm—I'll get you that chocolate."

"And cigarettes?"

"No cigarettes," Milly said, shockingly solid. She ducked her head as she passed the girls, and only after she left did Frankie realize she'd tried to send them a smile.

Kate placed her book next to her pillow. The dust jacket was shiny, despite the wrinkled pages. It boasted the latest knowledge about top cat breeds. It didn't seem like the kind of book she'd be interested in.

She nodded at Ivy's bandaged arm. "How are you doing?"

"It'll heal," Ivy said. They sat down, Ivy pulling her seat closer to Frankie's until their knees touched.

"And you?"

"Fine," Frankie said.

"Uh-huh." Kate shuffled up on her pillows, wincing as shifted her cast-heavy leg shifted. "What are people saying back in town?"

Ivy said, "Marvin's parents want an investigation into the, um, mysterious homeless woman who broke into the gym and. Uh. Killed him. And set the gym on fire."

"We'll get right on that," Kate said dryly.

If it had been anyone other than Ivy who did it, Frankie would have pushed Kate to follow it up. But manslaughter would still mean jail time. In this case, Frankie was A-okay with their town's habit of sweeping this shit under the rug. Even if she did feel bad for Marvin's parents. They were stuck-up jerks, but they deserved more than the bullshit story Kate coached the teenagers through before paramedics loaded her into an ambulance. It was the official story. Frankie didn't know how many people actually believed it. Most of Bulldeen High had seen April Tanner dead and see-through and bleeding in front of her screaming sister—but in true Bulldeen fashion, no one was talking about it.

Kate slumped back against the pillows. "Look, everything that went down—you should just forget about it. Move on. Don't even bother talking about it."

"A Bulldeen specialty," Frankie said. "How are you? Concussion gone yet?"

Kate rubbed the back of her head gingerly. "I'll be cleared to drive soon."

"And then out to—what, LA? What's in LA?"

Kate paused. "Milly's friends."

"Milly doesn't have any—" Ivy stuttered to a stop. Milly didn't have friends until last year, when she struck up a strange friendship with the Dead Freaks and the chief of police.

"She's staying," Kate continued. "I'm sticking around for a few days, saying hi. Then cruising through to Cincinnati."

Frankie asked, "What's in Cincinnati?"

The ceiling fan spun lazily overhead, circling cool air. For a moment it was the only sound in the room.

Kate rolled her tongue in her mouth. A soft smile spread over her face, something Frankie didn't think she was capable of. Then it was gone, the gruff expression locking back into place.

"Are they rebuilding the gym?"

Frankie snorted. "It burned down two years in a row. They'd be idiots to try."

Town officials had promised another rebuild—only half the gym burned down this time—but even they seemed unconvinced. It had been bad enough rebuilding the gym last year, and what use was a high school gym in a town that would be empty soon?

"Then we'll see," Kate said, toying with the corner of her book. The dust jacket bowed upwards. The real cover was as scratched and faded as the paper: *ROSIE'S TORRID LOVE*, the title claimed. Underneath, two women embraced, their dresses flowing against a cityscape. For a moment Frankie considered telling her about two girls under a flaming disco ball.

"Look. It's...nice of you girls to come visit. But I'm fine. You can head out," Kate said, and paused. "Parents driving you?"

"No. KJ. He's waiting in the car." Frankie got up. Considered thanking her. It seemed appropriate.

"See you," she said instead.

Kate's face turned grave. "I meant what I said. Forget what happened. Graduate. Go to New York. Go wherever the hell you want. Anywhere but here."

Frankie nodded. She was in the doorway, Ivy ahead of her and Milly a distant speck down the hall, when Kate called, "Girls?"

Frankie turned back. Kate was a white shape in the hospital bed. Frankie would never see her again. Still, she didn't say goodbye. Even with Kate's departure looming, even with Bulldeen's impending death, there was the innocent assumption most teenagers make: that they have more time.

Kate raised a hand. Even her fingers seemed older than they should, yellow with nicotine, wiry with the start of varicose veins.

"Nice necklaces," she said, and smiled.

KJ rubbed a constant, slow semicircle into the steering wheel. He'd been in the hospital that first night, comparing bite marks with Ivy. He was the one to ask why they weren't getting stitches, and the reason why they all learned that human bite wounds didn't get sutured, just bandaged: stitches made the risk of infection higher. The human mouth was a horrifying place.

"My parents are moving," he told the girls as they cruised toward Bulldeen twenty miles over the speed limit. He only kept one hand on the wheel, the other resting casually out the window, and both girls fought the urge to tell him to put his goddamn hand back on the wheel.

"We've got family in Ohio," he continued. "We'll head over after I graduate. Probably. I don't know, I don't love the idea of Ohio."

Frankie nodded. She didn't know the first thing about KJ's family, other than seeing his mom whisper soothingly to him during the tetanus shot. When the needle went in he'd buried his head in her shoulder. Frankie had politely averted her gaze.

KJ craned his head toward the rear-view mirror. The girls had spread out in the backseat.

"What about you guys? Your parents talking about it yet?"

Ivy rearranged her knees against the seat. She was lying in Frankie's lap, her head against her chest. "My parents are putting it off until I graduate."

KJ huffed. "Just gotta hope the school survives that long."

"Lotta people with lighters," Frankie muttered.

KJ huffed again. Cool-guy version of a laugh, Frankie supposed. She ran a gentle hand down Ivy's injured arm, curled against her chest. The bandages scratched gently at her fingertips. Time to redress them soon.

Frankie cleared her throat. "My parents had the talk with me last night, actually."

Ivy lifted her head. "Yeah?"

"Yeah. Dad's moving in a month. Mom's sticking around to see me graduate." Frankie didn't know who was more surprised: her, or her Mom, who had looked surprised even as she said it. What was more surprising: Dad had even mumbled about sticking around, moving to another house in Bulldeen for the next few years.

Since you're dealing with a lot, he'd said.

You don't know the half of it, Frankie had told him.

He didn't ask. Neither did Mom. Frankie was glad of it.

She sighed. "I don't know. Arson jokes aside, the thornfruit factory won't last another year. Who knows if Bulldeen High will last until we graduate?"

"Better last until *I* graduate," KJ said, checking his hair in the mirror. He flicked a flyaway curl back into place. "I'm not starting a new high school to finish the last year. Just...get a GED. People do that, right? Get the qualification, but not, like...go?"

Ivy was staring. Frankie knew it before she looked down to find those blue eyes aimed up at her, black lips glinting in the afternoon light. She'd borrowed Frankie's lipstick in the parking lot.

I'm thinking about incorporating it into my style, she'd said. *To match my neck.*

We'll make a goth out of you yet, Frankie had replied. Ivy had laughed, and for a second they were just two girls in a parking lot, no healing bites, no secret manslaughter, no sickly ash scent sticking to their hair.

"If it closes," Ivy said. "Even if it closes tomorrow, can we just—go to New York? Figure things out from there?"

Frankie wove their fingers together. Red on black. The nail polish was chipped, almost clear. They hadn't redone their nails since Homecoming.

"You got it," she said, and yawned.

KJ checked the car clock. "Barely into the ride. Still got time for a decent nap."

"I'm fine," Frankie said. She'd been sleeping much better since the dance. After the hospital she'd collapsed next to Ivy on her bed and slept for thirteen hours straight.

"We've got time," Ivy said.

Frankie kissed her forehead, wiping away the resulting black smudge. She pillowed her cheek on the top of Ivy's head, that lavender scent distinct even through the lingering smell of smoke.

Frankie breathed it in and fell into a dreamless sleep.

END.

sweethearts preview

Want to find out what happens next in Frankie and Ivy's story?

Check out book 3 in the BABYLOVE series: SWEETHEARTS.

zombabe preview

If you want to find out more about Babe, Dude and their friends, read on for more about ZOMBABE...

Bulldeen was dying.

For a long time, this place was a dump in rural Maine. The dump was cleared away during the 1860s, and the town of Bulldeen began. None of their crops survived that first winter. The next attempt clustered closer to town and held on long enough to harvest.

The changes crept in slowly, at first. People grew irritable, as was to be expected in those dire circumstances. Nobody was surprised when irritation turned to violence. After a few decades, the townsfolk started to sicken en masse. Kidney failure, seizures, brain damage.

An official diagnosis wouldn't come for generations, but the farmers knew then that the dump had turned the soil toxic. Everyone had eaten the slow poison, and so they made plans to start again, somewhere pure.

Then, in 1892, a miracle: a newcomer they would come to know as Founder Jim crafted a strange plant mutation he dubbed thornfruit. It thrived on the poison, sucking it from the soil and storing it in its stem. The fruit itself was sickly green, dangerously spiky, and disgusting. But it grew fast, and was safe to eat. For two years, it was their main food source. In 1894, it was discovered by a skincare company who ordered it by the boatload. The flesh of the fruit would be a key ingredient in moisturizers worldwide over the next century. Suddenly, the town glimpsed survival. An economy grew up around their miracle fruit, everybody ignoring the simple truth: this was a temporary fix. Thornfruit couldn't grow anywhere else. Many had tried to force it, but thornfruit thrived solely on Bulldeen poison, and there was a finite amount. When the last drop was leached from the soil, all those crops were going to rot. And Bulldeen would rot with it.

Henry "Babe" Simmons had never stepped foot outside of Maine. Two weeks before graduating in the class of 2003, he went over to watch TV with his best friend, Eugene "Dude" Marsh. Halfway through an impassioned argument about sweet breakfasts versus savory ones, Dude unknowingly gave him an Almond Delight chocolate bar containing traces of peanuts. After two squares, Babe's throat started to itch.

"I'm fine," he said, when Dude asked why he was clearing his throat so hard.

Thirty seconds later, his windpipe swelled shut.

He spent his last moments on his back, lying on Dude's carpet. In a pleasant moment at the end, he felt his panic subside, awash in endorphins that turned the world into one big, glowing aura. His hearing fizzing out and his vision pinholing, the world narrowed to his best friend's face swimming over him.

Dude was crying. Babe had never seen him cry before. It was beautiful.

"Babe," Dude begged.

Babe opened his mouth to answer, but lost consciousness. The paramedics charged into the room to find Dude pumping desperately on his chest, blowing into his cooling mouth. Thanks to the CPR, Babe had two broken ribs. He had been dead for twenty minutes.

This was a Wednesday.

On Sunday, he came back.

Babe's story continues in ZOMBABE!

thank you

Thank you so much for reading Sugarsnap!

If you want to support me, please leave a review on Goodreads, Amazon or any social media of your choice.

You can get updates on my upcoming LGBT YA books by subscribing to my newsletter! Sign up by visiting my website at isbelleauthor.com.

You can also follow me on Tiktok @i.s.belle_writes and Instagram @isbelleauthor.

acknowledgments

Special thanks to Jack McGee - you know what you did, you brilliant bald bastard.

Thank you to Catriona Turner and Edward Giordano for your editing work! Thank you to my beta readers for their feedback. And thank you to Laya Rose for the incredible cover art.

about the author

I. S. Belle is a Young Adult author who lives in New Zealand. She has a Creative Writing Masters from the International Institute of Modern Letters. She works in a bookstore and stops to pat dogs in the street. If you have a dog and your local bookshop allows pets - for the love of booksellers, please bring them in.

also by i. s. belle

BABYLOVE SERIES

BABYLOVE

SUGARSNAP

SWEETHEARTS - Coming Soon

ZOMBABE

ZOMBABE

GIRLS NIGHT

GIRLS NIGHT - Coming April 2024

Printed in Great Britain
by Amazon